Praise for Jim Grimsley

"His is a unique voice . . . always compelling us, as readers, as audience, to enter his world for a time."
—*Southern Voice*

"There are few writers who sustain our attention through tone and voice. Jim Grimsley belongs in this elite group."
—Fred Chappell, *Raleigh News & Observer*

"His writing is both thoughtful and thought-provoking. His books are wrenching stories, magnificently told."
—*Just Out*

Praise for *Dream Boy*

"Another potential award-winner. . . . Romantic passion, violence, and ultimate liberation coalesce in this singular display of literary craftsmanship."
—*Publishers Weekly,* starred review

"A powerful work that . . . leaves us with a powerful flavor and a flow of admiration."
—Fred Chappell, *Raleigh News & Observer*

"Grimsley proves once again that he can create believable characters and poignant situations that are resonant and heartfelt."

—*Winston-Salem Journal*

"*Dream Boy* is a powerful, fantastic novel."
—*The Columbia State*

"A tender . . . work of the soul that places Grimsley in the hallowed company of Baldwin, Carson McCullers in the school of emotional verisimilitude, and renders his story one to finish reluctantly and to part from never."
—Lawrence Schubert, *Detour* Magazine

"*Dream Boy* is unforgettable."
—*The Southern Pines Pilot*

"Superbly written . . . Grimsley writes with such quiet delicacy."
—*Detroit Free Press*

"Powerful."   —Elissa Schappell, *Vanity Fair*

"A strange and haunting work with uncommon tenderness . . . readers will be drawn by Grimsley's translucent prose and emotional authenticity."   —Tom Beer, *Out* Magazine

"One of the best novels of 1995 . . . at times incredibly erotic and arousing, at others heart-poundingly frightening. . . . An exquisite novel."   —Gregg Shapiro, *Gay Chicago* Magazine

"An intense lyrical narrative that explores the psychic intersections of love, sex, fear, violence, and repression."
                                    —Richard Morrison, *Independent Reader*

Praise for *Winter Birds*

"Remarkable . . . the story hits you in the gut."
                                    —Michael Skube, *Atlanta Journal-Constitution*

"Tell everyone, I have rarely read anything as powerful. *Winter Birds* is altogether marvelous, so beautifully written I wanted to steal it and pretend it was mine, or go on tour reading it aloud so people could hear how getting it right makes your both hurt and happy, makes you cry out loud and sing praises simply that we are human."
                                    —Dorothy Allison, author of *Bastard Out of Carolina*

"A story that blisters the sensibilities and shreds the heartstrings."
                                    —Susan Lynne Harkins, *Orlando Sentinel*

"Extraordinarily vivid . . . written very close to the senses. The sights, sounds, smells, and feel of the country are wonderfully realized."
                                    —Katharine A. Powers, *The Boston Globe*

"The violence is just half the story. The other half is the poetry that infuses *Winter Birds*. . . . A white-trash Southern landscape viewed from a gay perspective, with the bitterness of memory but also with unwavering, unsentimental love."   —*The New Yorker*

Also by Jim Grimsley
Winter Birds

Dream
Boy

Jim Grimsley

Scribner Paperback Fiction
Published by Simon & Schuster

SCRIBNER PAPERBACK FICTION
Simon & Schuster Inc.
Rockefeller Center
1230 Avenue of the Americas
New York, NY 10020

First Scribner Paperback Fiction edition 1997
Published by arrangement with Algonquin Books of Chapel Hill

SCRIBNER PAPERBACK FICTION and design are trademarks of Macmillan Library Reference USA, Inc. under license by Simon & Schuster, the publisher of this work.

Designed by Bonnie Campbell
Manufactured in the United States of America

5 7 9 10 8 6 4

Library of Congress Cataloging-in-Publication Data
Grimsley, Jim, date.
Dream Boy / by Jim Grimsley.
p. cm.
1. Fathers and sons—Southern States—Fiction. 2. Gay teenagers—Southern States—Fiction. 3. Teenage boys—Southern States—Fiction. 4. Abusive men—Southern States—Fiction. 5. Southern States—Fiction. I. Title.
[PS3557.R4949D74   1997]
813'.54—dc20   96-8237
CIP

ISBN 0-684-82992-4

For Frank Heibert

Dream Boy

Chapter One

On Sunday in the new church, Preacher John Roberts tells about the disciple Jesus loved whose name was also John, how at the Last Supper John lay his head tenderly on Jesus's breast. The preacher says we do not know why the Scriptures point to the disciple, we do not know why it is mentioned particularly that Jesus loved John at this moment of the Gospels. He grips the pulpit and gazes raptly into the air over the heads of the congregation, as if he can see the Savior there. His voice swells with holy thunder, and, listening, Nathan's father leans forward in the pew with a vision of God shining in his eyes. He is thinking about salvation and hellfire and the taste of whiskey.

Nathan's mother is thinking about the body of Christ and the wings of angels. Her spirit lightens in the safety, the sanctity, of the church. Dark hair surrounds her pretty oval face. Light from the stained-glass window tints her skin.

Nathan thinks about the body of the son of the

farmer who owns the house Nathan's parents rented three weeks ago. Jesus has a face like that boy, a serene smile with dimples, a nose that's a little too big, and Jesus has the same strong, smooth arms.

Preacher John Roberts says, "Let us pray," and Nathan bows his head with all the rest. With his eyes closed he pictures his family, father, mother, and son, neatly arranged in the church pew. The prayer means the sermon has ended, and the tautness in Nathan's midsection eases a little. The first day in the new church is over. Now everyone can stop staring. Dad, as if thinking the same thought, stirs restlessly in the pew. Mom sighs, dreaming of a Sunday morning that will never end.

Nathan pictures Jesus's hands spread against the wood of the cross, fine bones and smooth skin awaiting the press of the nail, the first moment of blood.

At the end of the service, the preacher stands at the door and shakes hands with the congregation as they leave. Nathan and his parents join the line. Various people from the congregation welcome them, so glad to have you, make sure you come back now, you'll like this church, there's good people in it. Dad has already been invited to the Men's Prayer Circle on Tuesday nights and the Deacons' Breakfast on Saturday morning. This will add nicely to Wednesday Prayer Meeting, Sunday evening Training Union, and the Thursday meeting of the Rotary Club.

After church, during the silent drive out of the town of Potter's Lake in the aging Buick, Nathan waits breathlessly. They have a house in the country this time, a farmhouse that stands adjacent to its more modern successor, at the end of a dirt road near what the local people refer to as the old Kennicutt Woods. The farmhouse and farmyard are neat and well kept, and the property includes a pond, a meadow, and an apple orchard. The farm family, Todd and Bettie Connelly and their son Roy, lives in the new house next door. They are back from church too, and Roy has already changed from his Sunday clothes and stands in the farmyard, hosing clay off his rubber boots beside the barn. Red clay has stained his white tee shirt, a smear the color of dried blood. Nathan tries not to stare, but Roy is two years older, and has the added prestige of being a school bus driver and a member of the baseball team. Roy catches him watching. He hesitates a moment, as if he too is waiting for a sign to speak. He nods his head in greeting.

All afternoon following Sunday dinner, Dad sips moonshine whiskey and reads from the Old Testament, the books of Kings and Chronicles. He is always quiet when they move to a new town. Nathan can rest easy today. Mom keeps Dad company in the shadowed living room at the front of the house. She is doing needlepoint, stitching the Alcoholic's Creed across cream-colored cloth. Embroidered violets climb the bases of each letter. As she stabs the needle through the cloth in the circular frame, she keeps her eye on Dad. When Nathan passes by, she offers him a wan smile. He returns it. But there is always the moment when she cannot look him in the eye any longer. She searches her sewing basket for thread. Nathan climbs silently up the narrow stairs.

His bedroom in the new house seems airy and spacious after the smaller rooms he has occupied before. Large windows face the Connelly house over the high privet. A figure in the upstairs window above the hedge draws Nathan's eye.

Roy stands there. Maybe that is his bedroom, where the pale curtains fall against his shoulder. He has stripped off the dirty tee shirt and leans against the window frame. He has a smile on his face and a self-conscious look in his eyes, as if he knows someone is watching. The curled arm is posed above his head. He moves away from the window after a while. But Nathan goes on waiting in case he comes back.

Roy has been watching this same way for a while. In the beginning Nathan thought he was imagining things. The first morning he rode the school bus, he thought it was unusual to find Roy studying him from the rearview mirror. They had barely said good morning when Nathan climbed onto the bus the first time, and yet here was Roy watching.

Sometimes the look in Roy's eyes reminds Nathan of his own father, of the look in his own father's eyes, but Nathan prefers not to think about that and shuts off the thought before it begins.

On the Monday morning after that first church service the sky unfurls its gray wash over the flat country, mist adrift over the fields beyond the Connelly house. Nathan wakes early and steps to the window. The partly open sash admits crisp morning air. Yellow light burns in

Roy's room. In the yard the muted school bus is parked beneath a pecan tree, brown leaves drifting across the orange hood. Nathan dresses with care, sliding a shirt over his pale body, buttoning buttons with lingering fingers, standing near his window so he can watch the other window. Now and then Roy's shadow crosses the visible wall.

After breakfast Nathan hurries to the bus. Roy waits in the driver's seat with sullen wariness. He speaks, for the first time going beyond a hoarse greeting. "I'm glad you're early, I like to leave a little bit before I'm supposed to," he says, and blushes and closes the door as Nathan takes the seat behind him. It is as if Nathan is drawn down into this seat by Roy's voice. They sit in silence, and Nathan watches the back of Roy's head. A line of red rises above Roy's collar, then subsides. Something has happened; Nathan puzzles at what it might be.

He feels as if there might be more. There is a kind of hidden movement in Roy, as if words are rising and falling in his throat. He races the engine of the bus and checks the play of the gear shift. Then, with an almost visible surrender, he abandons words and turns and looks at Nathan, simply looks at him.

"What is it?" Nathan asks.

"Nothing." Turning at once, Roy maneuvers the groaning, lumbering bus out of the yard.

The early ride is silent. There are no other families along the dirt road, called Poke's Road, that leads away from the farm. Even when other children climb aboard,

Nathan watches Roy, the curve of his shoulders and the column of his neck. Roy steers the bus neatly on its tangled route. After their arrival at school, Nathan is the last to leave the bus. Roy has already begun sweeping the long aisle.

This new school has required the usual adjustment. It is Nathan's second school since the fall term started, though Mom says they will live here for a while. Dad has made promises this time, she says. Nathan has gotten used to moving and hardly believes this time will be different. So here at school he is the new face again, sitting alertly in his desks in the various classrooms, answering the usual questions. *We used to live in Rose Hill and then my dad got a job where he moves around, he's a salesman, he sells farm equipment, he works in Gibsonville now. We live near Potter's Lake on Poke's Road. We live next to Roy and his folks.*

He remains serene. Already there are faces that he recognizes in each of his classes. Some of them have already heard from the teachers, who have heard from the guidance counselors, that Nathan skipped third grade in Rose Hill. That Nathan is very bright. The morning classes pass quickly, but then comes lunch, which is harder. He has been eating lunch at a table with kids he met in his sophomore Spanish class. He is not sure if he's welcome, but at least they do not chase him away. But at lunch this day, when Nathan heads for the table with his tray, suddenly Roy appears across the dining room.

Nathan sits, quietly. Roy wanders with his own lunch tray toward the same table. He studies the rest of the cafeteria with a troubled scowl, as if it is very crowded. Burke and Randy are following him in some confusion, since this is not their usual territory. Roy swings into a seat across from Nathan but at a slant from him. He glances at Nathan as if only seeing him at that moment. "Hey, Nathan."

His presence surprises the kids from Spanish. Roy is a senior and he hangs out with older kids who smoke on the smoking patio, like Burke and Randy, who are now making jokes about Josephine Carson and the black mustache on her upper lip, visible across the room. When Roy laughs, the deep timbre of his voice makes Nathan shy. In the watery light of the lunchroom, Roy's face seems full and strong, his nose almost in the right proportions. He goes on eating solemnly. Nathan fumbles with his fork. "You like your new house?" Roy asks.

"It's nice. I have the whole upstairs."

"We used to live over there. That room you got was my bedroom. Then Dad built us a new house." Something uncomfortable stirs at the back of Roy's eyes. He stares with seriousness at the plastic, sectioned plate.

With this remark, Roy has somehow included Nathan in the group with his other friends. Burke glances at Nathan as if wondering who he is, but he goes on sitting next to Nathan without comment, propped on thick elbows. As Nathan listens, the boys talk about their weekend at the fishing camp at Catfish Lake where a lot of high-school kids go to park or to get drunk. Burke drank too much beer this past Saturday, and pulled off all his clothes and ran up and down the lake shore whooping and hollering.

"You like to get drunk, Nathan?" Roy asks.

"Not much."

"That's because you're younger than us," Roy says. "I don't like it much either. It gives me a headache."

"You're full of shit, too," Burke says.

"Naw, I mean it. I drink a little bit, but it don't mean that much to me."

Nathan eats and stands. Roy has cleaned his plate too, then pushes it away and stretches. As if by accident he follows Nathan with his tray to the dishwasher's window.

There, Roy says he wants a smoke. He says this as if he has always included Nathan. Behind, Randy and Burke are scrambling to follow.

On the smoking patio, Randy, plump, round, and blond, addresses Nathan familiarly. Burke remains hidden, as if he hardly realizes Nathan is present at all. Some of the girls on the patio seem to notice Roy in particular, but he pays no special attention to anyone. Roy is famous for having a girlfriend at another high school, an achievement of real sophistication for a boy his age. He lights a cigarette, propping one foot on the edge of the round brick planter, which overflows with cigarette butts. His smoking a cigarette makes him seem harder, more aloof to Nathan, who stands beside him trying to look as if he belongs. Fresh wind scours the fields, stripping away layers of soil. Roy stands at the center of his friends; they are talking about deer-hunting season. Burke's Dad bought him a new rifle, a Marlin 30-30. Roy has a different type. They discuss the guns casually. They talk about going camping in the Kennicutt Woods. None of the talk includes Nathan, who owns no gun, stalks no deer. But with an occasional glance, Roy holds Nathan in place, without explanation.

When Nathan walks away from the courtyard at the sound of the lunch bell, he carries a cloud of Roy. He is distracted during his afternoon classes. Because of his scores on standardized tests, he is taking math and English with kids in the junior class during the afternoons. That day he has a hard time paying attention; he is thinking of Roy with the cigarette drawling from his lip. The math teacher asks if Nathan is sick at his stomach, he has such a pained expression on his face. The older kids, who are resentful of Nathan's presence, find the question funny.

At the end of the day, Nathan hurries to the bus, nevertheless too late, even after rushing, to claim the seat behind Roy. He is only temporarily disappointed. During the course of the ride, he works himself gradually forward, empty seat by empty seat, confident of eventual success since he will be riding to the last stop. Roy, efficient, steers from one dirt driveway to the other, and the orange bus discharges its passengers in clusters of neat frocks and clean blue jeans. Only two riders remain by the time Roy steers right at Hargett's Crossroads: a mumbling brunette girl named Linette, wearing blue butterfly barrettes, and an older black girl with bad skin, who sits directly behind Roy and talks to him every so often. Pretty soon the mumbling Linette steps out of the bus beside her mailbox, and within moments so does the girl with pocked skin. He and Roy ride alone on the bus to Poke's Road and all the way home.

Now that the moment has come, Nathan sits, stupefied. He gauges the few remaining empty seats between him and Roy. Roy glances at him in the general surveillance mirror. Finally he says, "Why don't you come up here?"

The question echoes. Nathan moves behind the driver's seat. A slight flush of color rises from Roy's collar. Nathan leans against the metal bar behind Roy's seat and hangs there, chin to seat back. The orange bus lumbers down the dirt road.

The feeling is restful. They can be quiet together. Nathan is glad, and wishes Poke's Road were longer.

Roy parks the bus beside the barn and sits for a moment. His face has taken on a strange meaning for Nathan, registering expressions Nathan would never have expected from someone older. Roy listens acutely, as if for some signal. It is as if he needs something but he cannot speak about it. Nathan lingers too, taking a long time to stack his books, straightening them carefully and arranging them largest to smallest. Roy says, reaching for his own books, "I have so much stuff to do on top of my homework, I'm about to go crazy."

"You have to work?"

"I got chores for my dad. There's always something to do around here." Roy grimaces, gathering his tattered notebooks and light jacket. "And I got to write a paper in English, and I don't want to."

"I'm good at that kind of stuff."

"Are you?"

"I like English."

"Then I'll come over later and you can help me. It's about railroads. The paper is."

Nathan can hardly believe the offer. Why does Roy want to spend time with him? Roy lets him descend first, but they linger on the short walk to the house. Roy says maybe he can help Nathan with other stuff, like math, since he's pretty good at math. Since Nathan is ahead of kids his own age, maybe he could use somebody older to help him. He mentions this casually, like a stray thought. They will study together later, after supper, the fact is established. Something about the agreement makes Nathan happy and afraid at the same time.

An image of his father gives the fear. The image comes to Nathan from dangerous places, from territories of memory that Nathan rarely visits. The memory is his father standing in a doorway, in the house in Rose Hill, and it reminds him of Roy because of the look in his father's eyes.

Later, standing at his bedroom window, Nathan watches Roy moving from barn to shed, shirt unbuttoned, sleeves rolled above his elbows, flesh bright as if the glow from a bonfire is radiating outward through his torso and limbs. He is cleaning the barn, stacking rusted gas cans and boxes in the back of the pickup truck, forking soiled hay into damp piles. He moves effortlessly from task to task as if he is never tired. The sight of him is like a current of cool water through the middle of Nathan.

It is a new feeling, not like friendship. Not like anything. Nathan has had friends before, especially before the family began to move so often. This feeling is stranger, forcing Nathan to remember things he does not want to remember.

After a while Nathan retreats from the window, lying across the bed scribbling idly at homework. He wants supper to be over. The arithmetic figures waver meaninglessly on the pages of his text. When he tries to concentrate, the word problems make periodic sense. He reads one long paragraph, considers it, realizes he has remembered nothing he has read, then finally stands, pacing to the window and drawing the curtain carefully back.

Roy stands below. He is waiting near the hedge as if he has called Nathan. He carries a wooden crate full of Mason jars with dusty, cobweb-covered lids. Nathan parts the curtains slowly. Roy waves hello without fear or surprise. Nathan fights the impulse to turn away, to pretend he has come to the window for some other reason than to look at Roy. Roy's gentle smile disturbs Nathan deeply. It is as if he knows what Nathan is thinking and feeling. He sets the crate on the back porch and turns. He heads back to the barn for more jars. Nathan goes on watching as long as there is light.

Mom calls Nathan to supper, and he descends from upstairs as if into some shadowy pool. He sits underwater and eats the food his mother has prepared. Tonight, Dad misses supper, working late. Tonight, Nathan can taste what is in front of him.

After supper, Roy crosses the yard to Nathan's house for help with his homework. Nathan sits at the desk in his bedroom with light from a warm study lamp pouring over his grammar textbook. He has completed work on his sentence diagrams. Footsteps sound in the hall, and when Nathan turns, Roy is leaning against the door jamb, gripping school books as if he would like to crush them in his big-boned hands. He says, "I told you I was coming."

"I know. I was waiting."

The statement pleases Roy. "You sure it's okay?"

"I finished my homework while you were doing your chores."

He has bathed and wears a white cotton shirt, buttoned to the collar. The cloud of his aftershave is vigorous. "Miss Burkette says you're supposed to be good at English, even if you are younger than me." He takes careful steps into the room, laying his books on the bed and rubbing his knuckles. "I hate to write stuff."

"I like it okay."

"I have to write about trains." Roy's brows knit to a sharp black line. He spreads open his notebook on the bed, and Nathan sits beside him on the sloping mattress. Miss Burkette has assigned his class to write a seven-paragraph essay on a preselected topic, "Railroads in the United States." Roy has brought the volume "Q–R" of the *World Book Encyclopedia* with him, and he shows Nathan

13

the sentences he has copied down from the article on "Railroad."

Nathan studies the writing and asks questions about the facts for the essay. Under these circumstances it becomes simple to talk, and the conversation feels as easy as their quiet. They discuss the essay seriously, agreeing that Roy must narrow what he wants to say about railroads, weighing one topic against another. Roy selects steam engines as a starting point and soon he is writing words on paper under Nathan's supervision. Roy seems vaguely surprised that the essay is actually getting written, and they work step by step through all the necessary decisions.

Mom brings iced tea for both of them, flushing when Roy thanks her, as if the acknowledgment is too much. She moves as if she would like to be invisible, same as she always moves, and yet she is clearly curious about Roy. When she retreats downstairs, they take the iced tea as a signal to rest. The evening is almost balmy. Nathan opens the window and takes long breaths. Roy stands, stretching. He sips tea and watches the half-finished page on the bed, thoughtful and quiet. "I guess I ought to be embarrassed, getting a kid like you to help me with my homework."

Nathan answers, fervently, "I take English with the juniors. That's just one year behind you. I'm not a kid."

Roy appears confused by what he has said. He blushes a little and reconsiders. "I didn't mean it bad. I mean you're younger than me, that's all." His gentle expression kindles. He approaches closer, and his nearness brings a physical reaction to Nathan, a sudden heaviness, as if his body is sliding toward Roy's. Roy goes on talking with calm ease. "I appreciate the help."

"I like to do it."

"You're pretty smart, aren't you? That's what everybody says. I mean, I'm not dumb or anything. But you're different."

He offers no response. But Roy goes on smiling. "We could be buddies, Nathan. You think so?"

His throat is dry and he is suddenly terrified. "Yes. I'd like that."

"You'll like living out here. In the summertime it's real peaceful. Nobody comes around."

"Is it okay to walk in the woods?"

Roy laughs as if the answer is self-evident. "Yeah. I go out there all the time. There's some great places, Indian mounds and camping places and a haunted house and stuff. I'll show you."

"I bet you have a lot of work to do in the summer. Because it's a farm."

"Yeah, but it's all right. It's all outdoor stuff and I like that. You ever live on a farm before?"

"No. We lived in towns before, mostly. But my dad wanted to live in the country this time."

"Why did you move here? Nobody moves to Potter's Lake."

Nathan can feel himself reddening. "My dad got a job. At the Allis Chalmers place in Gibsonville."

He is momentarily afraid that maybe Roy has heard some gossip. A breeze stirs Roy's fine black hair. The lamplight traces one arched brow and outlines a lip, a curve of jaw, a shadowed cheek. He would be handsome if it were not for his nose. Maybe he is handsome anyway. He sees Nathan watching and likes being watched; he squares his shoulders and clenches his jaw. "You like this school stuff, don't you?"

"I guess so. Most of the time."

"I don't see how anybody could like school."

"Beats staying at home all the time," Nathan says, and Roy laughs quietly. He leans toward Nathan. Nathan's breath hovers between them both.

"So you stay at home too much, huh? We can fix that."

They sit quietly in the aftermath of this implied promise. The sense of closeness between them survives the return to work. Roy finishes the paper and stays to copy it over. His handwriting is neat and square, an extension of his blunt hands. After he folds the paper neatly for safekeeping and places it inside his English book, he stays to talk about kids at school, about Randy who put jello mix in Miss Burkette's thermos of ice water, and Burke who beat up a Marine five years older than him at Atlantic Beach last summer. He talks about what it was like in Potter's Lake before integration and avows that the black kids are okay if you get to know them. He talks about baseball. He says he doesn't want to go to college but his folks want him to. He talks more than he has talked in a long time, he says as much himself, with an air of slight surprise.

At last Nathan's mother calls upstairs to remind them

it's about bedtime, and Roy stands. He tucks in his shirt and combs his hair at Nathan's dresser. His bundle of books lies on the bed, and when he turns for it he passes close to Nathan, lingering long enough that Nathan notes the difference. He takes the books, and Nathan walks him to the head of the stairs. Roy descends into the murky lower floor and passes out the kitchen doorway.

Nathan waits at the bedroom window, quietly tucked into a fold of curtain. The rich yellow bar of Roy's bedroom light spills across the hedge, and Roy's shadow passes one way and then another, a long teasing interval, until finally Roy returns to his own window. He glows in the warm square of glass. At last he waves to Nathan and disappears.

Nathan remains at the window a little longer, breathless and numb, the memory of the evening wrapping him like a warm mantle.

Chapter Two

But the new ease has vanished by morning and Nathan wakes full of fear that Roy will dislike him today. Roy will discover that yesterday was an accident and should never have happened. Nathan dresses with deliberateness and eats his breakfast slowly. The night was cloudy but morning is clearing, he notes the changing sky through the kitchen windows. He heads for the bus when he hears the engine running. The grass, heavy with morning dew, whispers to his feet as he crosses the yard. Roy waits in the driver's seat. He smiles when he sees Nathan, something shy in his expression. Nathan takes the seat behind him, and he hands back his books and asks Nathan to look after them. The books are warm and precious, placed in Nathan's trust. Roy grinds the bus into gear and commences the long drive to high school.

At lunch Roy finds Nathan again, setting his tray next to Nathan's, and announces that the essay, "Steam Engines in the U.S.A.," went over pretty big with his teacher. There is a message of gratitude behind the words, and Nathan savors it. Later Randy and Burke join them, and they tell jokes and dig elbows into each other's ribs. Nathan remains comfortable even in the presence of these other boys, and eats his lunch as he listens.

Randy strikes Nathan as curious at Nathan's sudden presence in their group. But he seems willing to accept. Burke hardly seems aware of anything, except occasionally Roy.

After lunch they head outside to the smoking patio, where Roy and the others smoke cigarettes. Roy says he thinks Nathan ought to go hunting with him and his friends sometime; even if you don't kill anything, hunting is fun, he says. Nathan studies Roy's lips on the thin cigarette, the place where the tender lip touches the filter, the compression of Roy's cheeks as he inhales. A bird wheels beyond his head in the clouds. The conversation continues the ease of the night before, and Nathan understands that Roy rarely talks so freely or on so many subjects. Roy declares he thinks it very practical to do your homework with somebody. The company makes it easier. This reminds him of his algebra class, where the senior class is studying something about the values of X and Y. Nathan listens attentively. Roy asks if he knows about solving equations for the unknown, and Nathan answers, truthfully, no. Tonight, Roy says, he will teach Nathan about it, as a way of paying Nathan back for the help on the railroad essay.

During every class for the rest of the day, Roy inhabits Nathan's mind, surrounded by whiteness and emptiness. It is perfect to think of Roy and nothing else, to dwell on Roy's image and think nothing at all. Roy will teach Nathan algebra, and Nathan will study Roy's shoulders and arms. The thought makes Nathan's mere arithmetic seem tedious and small. He stares at the flaked paint and rust on the iron posts that support the canopy outside. The clock spitefully crawls. Mr. Ferrette scratches the blackboard with fevered chalk. He occupies a fraction of Nathan's mind.

On the bus home Roy remains quiet, almost somber. Nathan sits behind him again but this time there is some change. Roy faces the bright world beyond the windshield. The very set of his shoulders denies any knowledge of Nathan. Nathan accepts the fact quietly. Fields wash by the windows, the motor roaring and groaning as Roy shifts gears with strong, sure motions. When he drives the bus to the back of the yard, under the pecan tree, he still stares straight ahead. A warning is evident in his quiet; Nathan presses for no attention. In the yard under the spreading pecan branches, Roy waits while Nathan gathers his books and hurries out of the bus, mumbling a good-bye that is barely returned. He does not ask whether Roy will come to his house tonight. Breathless, discomposed, he flies through the kitchen past Mom's flowered skirts (in which she is still studying how to be invisible) through the cloud of Dad's cigarettes (where he is already vanishing in the television's blue aura). Nathan climbs the stairs to his room and closes the door behind him.

Supper comes and goes. Nathan finishes his homework at the desk, from which he can see the lighted square of Roy's window. Now and then Roy's shadow passes the bright frame. Nathan sits quietly over his books. He studies his math a while, hardly concentrating, until he hears footsteps on the stairs.

When the door opens Roy is holding his algebra book before him like a shield. He grips the cover, which features a series of black and purple triangles on a field of burnt sienna. Roy's expression makes Nathan immediately cautious. "I told you I was coming over. Did you forget?"

"No." Nathan stands.

"Can I come in?"

"Sure."

Roy enters and cautiously sits on the bed. He sets out his books in a way that designates a place for Nathan beside him. The math book falls open. Soon Roy is writing in his firm hand on the notebook beside Nathan's thigh. He denotes equations in letters and numbers, illuminating each in pencil as he describes their arcane meanings and functions. Roy speaks to Nathan as to a peer and not as to a younger boy. Algebra is simple. You learn to work from both sides of the equation, to find the answer implied by circumstance. He sets out problems that become increasingly clear, reading from the math book about the price of yellow and green ribbon in Mr. Sawyer's department store, about the number of nickels in $1.97 if there are four quarters and six dimes. Finding a solution for the problem, as Roy explains it, requires a peculiar and inexorable logic. Enlightenment comes to Nathan at the

Jim Grimsley

same time that Roy's presence begins to have its usual effect on him. The principles of algebra break over Nathan like day. What has not before been known—the undiscovered element in any circumstance—may be ferreted out, exposed to light. Nathan watches Roy's hands on the pages, his brows knit together as he reads. There is an unknown here in this room. X and Y hang in the air between them.

Roy lets Nathan solve a word problem himself, leaning close to watch and explain. Again with his nearness comes that field of magnetism that possesses Nathan. Roy watches calmly from his side of the equal sign. He has moved close now, his breath touches Nathan along the soft of the throat. No logic can explain such warmth. Roy sets down his pencil and Nathan touches the veins on the back of Roy's hand. The contact shocks them both. Roy is quiet. Shy, like Nathan. But neither hand moves.

Roy leans close till his forehead brushes Nathan's, dark hair tickling, his eyes downcast. The rhythms of their separate breathings merge into one river. No other sound intrudes as they lean against each other, skull to skull. Nathan feels the unknown rising in them both, its message plainer than either can fathom. Roy cups his warm hand against Nathan's neck. Roy's breathing deepens, reaches inside. Now both his hands are trembling.

Roy is starved for closeness. Nathan leans against him, since it seems it is warmth that he craves. But the effect is out of proportion; it is as if he has cracked Roy's shell. Roy makes a sound as if he is taking his first breath.

22

He pulls Nathan down to the mattress, unmindful of textbook and papers beneath. His weight is delicious and full. Their breathing changes together, and they press against each other, warmth exchanged for warmth, as Roy sighs into Nathan's hair.

In the quiet wake of the moment, the sounds of the house clarify and isolate themselves. Mom washes dishes in the subterranean kitchen. Dad dozes through the weekly Hawaiian detective series in the living room. Out in the world the wind is blowing leaf against leaf, an insistent whispering with a scent of storm. "Does this make you feel funny?" Roy asks.

"No."

"It makes me feel funny."

"Well, maybe it makes me feel a little funny too. But I don't care."

"I don't care either. I just wonder why." He lies on the bed watching the ceiling. "Do you like me?"

"Yes." Nathan can hardly lift his eyes from the soft chenille.

"Do you like me a lot?" There is something frightened in the question. Roy's body has become rigid. It is as if he is denying the words as they emerge.

Nathan speaks suddenly, with violence, against Roy's shoulder. "I like you a whole lot. I really do. And I want you to like me the same way."

"I do," he says. Saying so much has apparently surprised him; he stands from the bed adjusting his pants, asking if Nathan wants to walk outside away from the houses. In the dark. Nathan spares no breath for an answer but falls in beside him down the corridor, descending the back stairway to the kitchen, pausing while the shadow of Mom retreats into the dining room, the unknowable rooms beyond. At the back door Roy's hand hovers over Nathan's. Fresh air from the night spills over Nathan. Roy steps into the inky quiet and Nathan orbits him.

Mom's dim voice calls out, "Where are you going, Nathan? Nathan?"

"Outside." By then the night surrounds him.

Roy runs and Nathan follows, into the waist-high weeds behind the barn, into the flood of moonlight that pools within the pokeweed and broomstraw. Roy is laughing from deep inside his chest, and he runs ahead into the white, glowing world. Nathan follows at his slower pace. The twinned houses dwindle behind, and the shadow pines rise up toward the stars. Nearing the pond, they descend the slight embankment leading to the watery lip. Roy pauses at the edge, touching his sneaker to the waterline. He checks to make sure Nathan is following, then kneels with a sycamore branch, drawing a line in the pale muddy pond bottom. The moonlight records the motion perfectly, they can see everything. Clouds of mud rise in the water from the tip of the stick.

"I like this place at night."

Nathan stops near Roy's elbow. "It's quiet."

"There's a cemetery over yonder." Roy points with the stick. To a thickening of shadow.

He shivers. "A real one?"

"Yeah. With great big tombstones. There's a lot of them, with angels and statues. They look pretty spooky at night."

"Can we go there?"

"You sure you want to? Your mom might get mad if we stay out too long."

"I want to."

Willows, arrow arum, and cattails grow to the edge of the pond, and royal fern and honeysuckle overhang the glimmering water. Branches crack underfoot, pine needles protesting. Roy's passage is quieter than Nathan's, his feet somehow lighter. He lifts aside limber branches with an easy hand, holding them over Nathan's head. The path through the darkening trees is washed with light, and the substance of Roy moves through it dense and shadowed. Nathan hurries behind Roy, drawing audible breath after audible breath. The pond spreads a hush, the trees lift their branches, the stars and moon burn. Between is a blackness the eye fails to fathom.

The cemetery gate and iron fence form out of nothing, within a circle of trees at the top of a rise of land. Roy opens the iron gate and shows Nathan the rust stains on his palms. The two are silent as they move into the enclosure, overgrown with weeds. Tombstones, some top-pled, and the leavings of wreaths impede their passage. The ground gives off a clotted, dank smell. Roy is breath-less. He passes his hand along eroded marble in which let-ters are carved. Nathan studies the words but fails to read them, so Roy leans close and whispers, "This one says,

Sarah Jane Kennicutt, Her Father's Favorite Daughter. The Kennicutts used to own all this land, that's what people say. There were two Kennicutt plantations, one right around here that burned down, and another one off in the woods."

"Then why is it Poke's Road?"

Roy shrugs. "Poke's Road goes for a long ways. It must have been some Pokes on it, once upon a time." He is leaning against Nathan. "I'll take you to the end of that road one of these days. Way off in the woods where it's overgrown and nobody can use it."

Nathan nods, but is rendered speechless by touch. Roy grips Nathan's arm and leads him to another grave over which looms a guardian obelisk. The shadow of the granite shaft passes across Roy's face, and his expression is inscrutable. Something in Roy's stance lays a field of silence around them both.

Now both Roy's hands touch both Nathan's arms. He watches Nathan with a new quiet. It is hard for Nathan to be conscious of anything but the touch of those hands on his arms, the texture of tough skin and strong fingers. Nathan makes one sound, throaty and startled, like an animal giving a single warning. Roy exerts the slightest pressure.

His body is full of curves beneath the clothes. Nathan leans against him, as Roy slightly smiles. He kneels in the grass and brings Nathan down with him. The two are trembling and huddle together in the dark of the grave.

The sweetness of the moment lingers. The salty smell of Roy's body rises out of the shirt that he unbuttons and slides over his shoulders. Moonlight glitters on the slight sweat of his chest. A calm deliberateness engulfs him. Nathan eases the worn jeans down Roy's thighs. Air pours against Nathan's skin as Roy strips away his cotton tee shirt. Nathan shivers with the chill.

Roy embraces the slighter boy and their warmth multiplies, their bodies shuddering and yet clinging each to the other, dressed only in white underwear in the shadow of the granite marker. The warmth makes chromosomes sing. Roy says, "Now we're buddies," with a tone of deep relief in his voice, and Nathan mouths the words soundlessly, watching the North Star over the pond. He wonders what a buddy is and whether he is the only one Roy has. He is farther from home than he has ever been. Roy cradles him as if he will never let go. "Bats fly around here sometimes. You can hear them making that squeak noise."

"Do you hear any now?"

"No. I don't hear anything except you. But this is the place for bats, ain't it?" Roy surveys the surrounding tombstones as if they are his estate. He talks about them quietly as Nathan rests against him. "This thing is called an obelisk," he explains, and Nathan pretends to learn this as a new fact. "It's something people in the old times would put on a grave. This grave belongs to Frederick Kennicutt. He was kin to my great-grandaddy."

Nathan knows nothing about his own great-grandaddy. He simply watches Roy mouth the words. "Come on."

They uncoil and creep quietly through the tombstones in their undershorts. Along a rise of land they climb, to a place where the black pond is visible below. Up there is a statue of a plump baby wearing a robe, with stubby marble wings sprouting from its shoulders. Roy stands large and shapely beside the angel-baby, Roy more radiant than the stone in the same fall of thin moon-and-starlight. The sight of Roy encumbers Nathan so that even his gaze feels heavy; Roy is like an immense gravity and he is pulling Nathan toward him without any effort. Again Roy yields to Nathan's hands, gives way to touch. Nathan bends his knees and Roy rests on the ground beside him, above him. Nathan is breathing into the hollow of Roy's collarbone and Roy is laughing softly, reasonless.

Roy brushes his mouth against Nathan's and Nathan is surprised. Roy's taste is sweetish, life rising out of his throat, hot as if from deep furnaces. He holds Nathan's delicate skull in his hand. Nathan resists nothing. He lies down on their clothes in the weeds beneath the marble child, and Roy lies down along him. Roy is content to be still like that for a long time, sometimes watching Nathan and sometimes not, his open hand on Nathan's face. Their legs tangle in the weeds. Nathan can see the distended fabric of Roy's shorts, but he does not touch the place directly and Roy abstains from asking. They lie together, heat fields enfolded, kissing awkwardly now and then.

Roy says, "When we do this, you can't tell your parents."

"I won't."

"You can't tell your friends either. This is a secret."

"I know." Nathan feels some desperation he cannot name, like a slow sob.

"I'm not your boyfriend." Roy rests against Nathan as before, but they have each become still. "I have a girl-friend. And I don't need to do this if I don't want to."

Nathan receives the words all the way to the center of his bones. He watches Roy's face, trying to see through to his mind. It is like the silence on the bus, this moment. It is like Roy squaring his shoulders to the front of the bus. They lie together for a long time. Nathan watches the pond with Roy's shivering belly under his hand. Roy's large thigh stirs in the grass. The crickets drone. Finally Roy says, in a tenderer tone, "We better get back."

Nathan stands and finds his clothes. Roy dresses close to him. The night has filled with sounds. From the shadows overhead come calls of night birds, and from the distant darkness echoes the yowling of a faraway cat, the singing of frogs, the murmuring of wind in branches. One shrill thin cry shivers along Nathan's spine, sounding almost human. A bobcat, Roy says.

In the backyard, in the shadow of the barn, Roy embraces Nathan, holding tight. "Bring my books in the morning. I'm going on home." No more parting than that. Roy's shadow vanishes.

In the kitchen, Nathan drinks sweet tea standing by the sink. The house is quiet except for the drone of the television.

Then Dad is in the room.

"Is that you son?"

Nathan sets the glass carefully, quietly, onto the sink. "Yes sir."

The sweetish smell of his Old Spice clouds the kitchen. He has come from the living room. He is standing in shadow. "You been out for a walk."

"Yes sir."

"Where did you go?"

"Out to the pond. There's a graveyard out there."

"Who did you go with?"

"Roy. Next door." Very softly.

"He's a nice boy," Dad says.

He comes forward into the light and Nathan backs away. He considers Nathan from beside the refrigerator. Dad is wearing his white boxer shorts with the stained front, his white tee shirt with the torn sleeve and cigarette burns. The whiteness of his flesh, the softness, make Nathan look away. "There's a Western on the TV. You ought to come watch it with your dad."

"No sir."

Dad ponders this. He opens the door of the refrigerator. "All right. Then go on to bed."

Nathan has been holding his breath. Released, he slips quietly upstairs, without turning on the light. He waits at the window until he is calm. He listens to make sure Dad goes back to the living room.

Across the yard Roy's window is dark. So it remains.

Chapter Three

In the morning, a heavy mist has settled onto the yard, and Nathan can hardly see the bus as he heads into the cloud zipping his jacket. His own books and Roy's are crooked in his arm. The idling motor guides him to the haze of the yellow bus. Roy straddles the driver's seat gazing out the window at the dismal morning. He says nothing, closes the door and turns on the headlights.

The rutted road tosses Nathan from side to side on the seat. The inside of the bus is like the sky this morning, a silence condensing around every sleepy face. Everyone says good morning to Roy pleasantly, distantly. No hello is returned by Roy with any sign of hidden feeling. Nathan searches but finds no evidence of a girlfriend in these faces. But this thought hardly brings any peace. Nathan already knows Roy has a girlfriend at his church, and Roy goes out with her all the time.

At school Nathan leaves the bus with the first wave this time, letting Roy sit like a boulder. His coldness seems oddly expected. But Nathan remembers lying on their clothes in the cemetery, his hand on Roy's naked belly in the shadow of the obelisk. Roy will treat Nathan as he pleases, and Nathan expects the coldness. In the daylight Nathan will be invisible.

So at lunchtime Nathan sits away from Roy and his friends, at a table by the southern wall of windows, among the black kids. He drinks his milk and chews his macaroni and cheese. His mind, as he eats, is a perfect wash, free of any stray imagining. He avoids the smoking patio, after lunch, in favor of the lawn in front of the school, sheltered by the brick sign announcing FORRESTER COUNTY HIGH SCHOOL to the fields beyond. He sits in the shadow, hidden, and hums a hymn from church about the peace that passes understanding.

A new friend crosses the yard beyond, Hannah from Nathan's civics class. Hannah visits briefly, asking if Nathan is ready for the test on the American Constitution next week. Yes, Nathan answers. Hannah is pimpled and pleasant and talks for a while, idle and mundane chatter, but while she is there, Roy passes. His posture radiates anxiety, hands jammed into pants pockets, shoulders rigid. He sees Nathan and stands watching. He scowls and shoves his hands deeper.

Even now, even from this distance, his body draws Nathan toward it, and Nathan stands to join him; but suddenly Roy storms away, shoulders hunched, frowning.

The afternoon chokes Nathan, sitting in hot, dark classrooms with windows no teacher will open. He sits through advanced math with his Venus pencil poised, paper glaring at him from the desktop. Mr. Ferrette crumbles chalk against the chalkboard. When the final bell rings and everyone hurries toward the buses, Nathan walks toward his own bus with a small fear inside.

Roy straddles his vinyl saddle watching the accelerator pedal on the floor, books loose in one arm. Others enter before Nathan does; he nods to them; Nathan is too far away to read Roy's expression; but when Roy sees Nathan he turns, making a production of settling his books into the basket beside the seat. Momentum carries Nathan to the back of the bus, where he sits, quietly watching the top of Roy's head in the rearview mirror.

The drive home is tedious and tense at the same time, the bus a senseless rattling contraption that sends up a cloud of stinking exhaust, vapid voices, and vacant laughter. Nathan props his knees against the seat in front, glaring at the ridged rubber mat that runs the length of the aisle. No matter where he looks, he can feel Roy's sullen anger at the front of the bus. Roy scans the highway with lips set in a line. Nathan clutches his books against his stomach, remembering the softness of Roy's cheek, the taste of his mouth.

The bus makes its usual stops, the bodies thinning among the seats. Soon there are only a few voices between Nathan and Roy. Again soon, Nathan sits alone in the back of the bus and Roy alone in front; Roy stares forward and Nathan stares downward, each with equal stubbornness. Roy turns the bus down the dirt road through the Kennicutt Woods. Nathan cannot help but watch the strong arms turn the wide steering wheel, while Roy remains oblivious and shifts gears with precise violence. But, past the first few curves of the road, he pulls the bus to the side and stops.

Nathan watches in surprise. Roy sags back against his seat, arms falling limp at his side. His deep breathing is audible. "I got a question for you."

Nathan voice sounds timid, small in the empty bus. "What is it?"

"What were you doing with that girl in the front of the school?"

Studying the back of Roy's head for a clue. The mirror is empty. "Nothing. I was just sitting there and she came up."

"Oh sure," Roy says.

"She's in my civics class. She was asking me about this test we got."

"What's her name?"

"Hannah something."

"Do you like her?"

"She's all right."

Roy's voice trembles a little. "Do you like her the way you like me?"

The question echoes into silence.

"No."

Roy sits still. Nathan's heart pounds and calm is hard to find. Roy stands. He stares at the rubber mat as he walks down the aisle. He is shaking as he kneels beside Nathan's seat. "I don't know if I believe you or not."

"I'm telling the truth."

"Touch me," Roy says, and Nathan embraces him. He leans against Nathan, who caresses the thick hair at the nape of his neck. He opens his shirt slowly and Nathan feels the strong upsurge of breath and desire, same as the night before; only in the daylight the rich color of his flesh glows, blinding, and when Nathan touches the curves and planes, the sudden rush of heat engulfs them both.

For Nathan it is a moment of poise, in which he must balance between what he knows and what he should not know. The fact of Roy makes a difference. Here it is easy to be held. Nathan's body has never felt so safe. They are touching each other in intimate places with a feeling of perfection. Their breaths, as they fumble and mingle, come faster; they cling and press until they finish. Nathan holds his eyes closed, aware of Roy against him and glad of the clean curved lines of Roy's body. Glad to lay his hands on Roy's firm shoulders and flat waist. The trembling of a vein in Roy's neck draws Nathan's fingers. The clean lines of Roy are a relief and Nathan focuses on that. Without reason, in Nathan's inner seeing, the vision of Preacher John Roberts arises, telling again how at the Last Supper John lay his head tenderly on Jesus' breast. Nathan ends that way, with Roy's fingers in his hair. Roy asks, "Did you ever do this before with anybody?"

Nathan shakes his head, unable to speak. He has never liked it before. That much is true.

"Do you promise?" Roy asks, and the fear is plain on his face when Nathan looks at him.

"I promise. I never did it with anybody." Hoarse, almost inaudible. Feeling hollow inside.

"Because it's okay as long as it's just you and me." Roy's face is suddenly very sad. Nathan reaches for the face, pulls Roy close. Roy settles, sighing, against Nathan's smaller shoulder. "I never did this much before. Not even with a girl."

Nathan holds him as if he has diminished. Nathan becomes the shelter, the protection. He touches Roy's chest with the tip of his tongue and Roy shudders; inside, his heart is regularly bursting. Stillness settles over the bus. Roy sighs and loops an arm around Nathan, keeping close to him through the aftermath, as the sinking sun caresses them through the windows.

When they can move again, Roy leads Nathan to the front of the bus, drives home down the twisting road with the shadows of the trees passing across his shoulders. He parks the bus in the usual spot in the yard and turns in the seat. "Don't go in yet."

"All right. I won't."

Roy studies his own hands, gripping the steel frame of his seat, smooth nail against smooth rivet. "I can't come to see you tonight. We have prayer meeting."

"At church?"

He nods. "Every Wednesday." He will not look up.

"Do you like to go?"

"Yes."

"I have a lot of homework to do anyway. I have a test. I told you."

But Roy has heard only his own thoughts. Lips parted, as if words are close, Roy glances toward his house. He leans to Nathan, kisses him quickly. Pulling on his shirt, he says he will see Nathan later and hurries away without a backward glance.

The night is long and Roy moves restlessly in Nathan's thoughts. Nathan studies mathematics slowly, solving his tedious, nonalgebraic problems with an indolent air. Later he walks to the pond, though not as far as the abandoned cemetery. He can see the distant outline of the tombstones against the black backdrop of trees.

He has gone to bed when Roy finally arrives at home again, driving his parents' car into the yard, letting it idle a moment. Nathan leaps out of the blankets. He stands back from the window to make sure Roy cannot see him. Roy steps out of the car, illuminated by the yard light atop its creosote pole. His figure is handsome in white shirt and tie, his face in shadow. Judging from his stance, he might be watching Nathan's window. But still Nathan hangs back, listening to the muted creakings of the house around him, the syncopated drip of water in the downstairs bathroom. Wind rattles the upstairs windows in their frames. Roy presently heads into the deeper gloom beneath trees, walking with his mother, who moves slowly due to her size. Nathan hovers in the dark over them both.

Soon a dim light burns in the bedroom above the hedge. As before, Roy's shadow slides across the visible wall. Tonight he avoids the window, and Nathan watches his shadow undress.

When that room goes dark, Nathan stands dumbly before his own window, reluctant to turn. When he returns to bed, a small fear seizes him. He replays in his head every moment of Roy's arrival, his stepping out of the car, his standing in the shadow, his undressing out of sight of the window. Nathan lies in bed and examines each of these images over and over. Something in the sequence of events frightens him.

Yet the following day proves to be all Nathan could have wished. In the morning he sits in the seat behind Roy again, and on the way to school Roy talks to him in an almost intimate way. At lunch Roy sits with Nathan and afterward takes Nathan to the smoking patio. No friend takes precedence over Nathan, and no girl excites his attention.

Only once, when Nathan asks about prayer meeting, does the little fear return. Roy says the meeting was fine but refuses to look at him. All further questions about Roy's church stick in Nathan's throat.

That afternoon, when Roy parks the bus under the pecan trees, he tells Nathan to hurry inside and change clothes, he wants them to go for a hike in the woods while there's still light. To an Indian mound, he says, beyond the pond and the cemetery. He grins and lets the bus motor die. The door hardly swings open before Nathan dashes for his house.

In the kitchen his mother stands at the sink washing a cake pan and icing bowl. The room shimmers with afternoon light, filtered through red-checked curtains, adding color to her face and hands. "I'm making a coconut cake. Do you want a little piece of layer?"

"No, ma'am. I'm not hungry."

"It's still warm out of the oven, it would be good."

"I'm not hungry for cake right now."

This disappoints her a little, but she goes on smiling warmly. "Well, did you have a good day at school?"

"Yes, ma'am."

"Well, sit down and talk to me about it. What are you in such a hurry for?"

"Roy wants me to change clothes and come out to the woods with him."

She studies her dishes and frowns. Her glistening hands move deliberately. "What does he want you to go in the woods for?"

"To see this Indian mound."

"What do you want with an Indian mound?"

"I never saw one before."

She looks out the window. "There he is, too, waiting on you."

"Can I go? Is it all right?"

She goes on watching Roy, her face filling with worry. "I guess you can. But I don't want you to go too far."

"Yes, ma'am, I won't."

"Remember, he's bigger than you are. You don't have to do everything he does."

"Yes, ma'am, I know."

She dries her hands and kisses Nathan's forehead without looking at him. "Put on your everyday clothes. I'll tell him you're coming."

Nathan rushes upstairs, furiously erasing his mother's sadness from his mind. When, school clothes exchanged for everyday, he returns to the porch, she is fussing with her plants, pinching a dead leaf off the ivory, wiping the leaves of a snake plant with a cloth. She says to be careful in the woods, don't stay gone too long. Nathan answers, yes ma'am, yes ma'am, and bursts into the yard. Roy awaits beyond the hedge. The two boys run side by side through the apple orchard.

The rhythm of running carries them a long way, beyond the meadow. They crash through underbrush but make no other sound. Leaves strike the skin of Nathan's arms, stinging and caressing. Roy leads him west of the pond and cemetery; he lopes deeper into the woods, glancing back to make sure Nathan is keeping up. Roy laughs at the glory of motion, a bright, incomprehensible sound that echoes through the woodland. He leaps across a narrow stream where drooping ferns make elegant green arches, and Nathan follows, light, running as if he will never tire.

The forest is something other than a neighbor now; it becomes a new world. As the density of growth increases, the pace of their running slows. Soon it is easier to walk than to run, and Nathan draws abreast of Roy. Roy gives a look that instructs, that says he is pleased. The Indian mound is pretty close once they cross the creek, he says.

The land is rising. Nathan climbs past bent saplings and red-leafed dogwood; Roy has run up the hill a little faster than Nathan and pauses, breathless.

The forest thins and light spills into the lower tiers of growth. Beyond a glade of trees, on a flat of land, a long mound rises. Only green grass grows on the mound, as if all other kinds of plants have been magically forbidden. Golden sunlight tumbles along the gentle slope.

Roy hangs his shirt from his beltloops. When Nathan does not follow suit of his own volition, Roy reaches for his shirt buttons.

The air, Roy's hands, light spilling down.

Roy offers Nathan the shirt, tenderness in his expression, then runs down the long slope. Nathan threads the sleeves through the belt loops of his pants and follows. Roy vanishes momentarily, but Nathan, heart pounding from the run, finds him. Roy is a strong silhouette against the bright mound, walking toward it. Nathan overtakes him halfway up the mound.

Nathan draws near shyly and Roy refuses to turn. Roy's back muscles shift in a rhythm that seems strong and good. The warm brown skin invites Nathan's hands, but he refuses to reach. They are still climbing. A curious fact, Roy's breath labors more than Nathan's. When on the crest of the mound Roy turns, his ribs are beating open and closed like wings.

Nathan lays his hand against the pounding in the cleft of Roy's chest.

Roy watches his hand, watches Nathan.

Jim Grimsley

Their two fleshes are bright together, the two boys, warm like the colors of the late sky. The sun still has some descending to do, and they watch it and the clouds for a while. Roy settles along the ground, spreading out his shirt, and Nathan does the same. Soon they are layered against each other. Roy says the movement of the treetops is like the ocean. Nathan knows nothing about the ocean; he listens to the murmuring of Roy's insides, the ferocious heartbeat that shakes through them both. Roy is murmuring in Nathan's ear, a hymn from church, "There is a place of quiet rest, near to the heart of God." Nathan sings too, kissing Roy's soft throat, his collarbones, the underside of his chin. He can smell Roy's body, he can taste it with the tip of his tongue. Roy grips the back of Nathan's head as if afraid he will escape. He need not worry. Nathan knows the nakedness Roy wants, and soon achieves it. Roy arches with his body toward Nathan, a curve of yearning. He lies bare in the grass with a look on his face as if Nathan is making him sing through every cell.

They lie still while the sun settles into the green bath of leaves. Roy says nothing but Nathan can feel how his spirit darkens. The banded sky begins to drain of color as they dress. Roy stands with his hands in his pockets. He calls, "Nathan," in a strangled voice and Nathan walks close; he brings Nathan's ear to his mouth and says, "Please don't say anything about this to anybody. Okay? Please."

"I won't." For a moment, just a little, Nathan is afraid. Roy has frozen with one leg in his pants, the other not.

"Is something wrong?"

"You just can't say anything about it. That's all." A bitter whiteness sheathing his expression. "It's near dark. We better get home."

But even then they linger in the forest. At first Roy holds Nathan's hand but later is ashamed or shy. Yet he refuses to hurry, walking slowly, never straying far. He brags that he knows all the land around his father's farm, he could find his way home in the pitch dark if he had to. Soon Nathan glimpses the cemetery through the trees, and then the pond, and they are walking along the tangled shore within sight of the backs of both houses. They slow their walking even more, and each reaches for ways to manage nearness to the other without seeming responsible for it. In back of the barn, Roy takes Nathan next to him, again furiously, as if the act makes him angry. "You can't do this with anybody but me. Do you hear what I'm telling you?"

Nathan's heart suddenly batters at them both. "I don't want to do it with anybody else."

"Just remember." Red-faced, Roy is already rushing toward his house.

Nathan wanders toward his own kitchen, hearing the sounds that indicate supper heading to the table. Already he is calculating the turns of the cycle, that tonight he will not see Roy, that tomorrow Roy will not say much on the bus. None of that makes him afraid, exactly. Nathan has no words for what does make him afraid. But he feels the chill of it as he descends into the house, where his mother has prepared a meal carefully but will hardly look him in

43

the eye, where his father brings the Bible and a tumbler of whiskey to the dinner table, mumbling verses under his breath as he takes his seat. In the submersion of home, Nathan returns again and again to the image of Roy's body on the Indian mound, lost and bewildered under the power of Nathan's mouth.

Chapter Four

Their guest for supper is Saint Paul, and the text is Romans, chapter one. Dad reads neither aloud nor silently, he chants softly as if he is alone, the words a stream of sound that barely rises above the gold-edged pages of God's holy word. *Because that, when they knew God, they glorified him not as God, neither were thankful; but became vain in their imaginations, and their foolish heart was darkened.*

The whiskey sits at his right hand, the knife and fork at the left. Today it is real whiskey bought from the local package store, not the clear moonshine of weekends and holidays.

Mom, restless, gives the appearance of hovering slightly above the seat of her chair. Neither listening nor speaking, she chews her food in a mechanical motion. As always at mealtime, she wears a frightened expression, glancing from Dad to Nathan, then fixing her attention on her plate.

Dad reads: *Professing themselves wise, they became fools, and changed the glory of the uncorruptible God into an image made like to corruptible man, and to birds, and to four-footed beasts, and creeping things.*

Nathan eats though he can hardly taste. When he sits at the supper table with Mom and Dad, the twisting of his gut is unrelenting, and every soft-spoken word from the King James Bible reverberates.

They are a family during certain mealtimes and during church. Each night, each Sunday, they eat together, because they always have. The repetition echoes darkly through the country of Nathan's memory, through all the dangerous territories in which his thought may no longer move freely. Through all that he has forgotten and locked away.

Once there was a younger Dad, of firm flesh and clear skin, a Dad who could look Nathan in the eye when they talked, who could drink his whiskey on the weekends and stay sober through the week, who could play ball with Nathan in the yard. Once there was a Dad without a soft belly hanging over his belt, without the slackness of this one's jaw or the broken veins in his cheeks and nose, a Dad whose eyes were not yellow-ringed-with-red. Once there was a man who could kiss Mom on the cheek with a clear heart, who could pick up Nathan in strong arms and toss him toward the ceiling like a toy. That other Dad remains, somewhere; but not here inside this pale body huddled over its gilt-edged Bible. The spider veins tracing Dad's cheeks and the yellow skin of Dad's hands are frightening to Nathan. There is even the smell of rot that underlies his father's sweet aftershave.

Being filled with all unrighteousness, fornication, wicked-

ness, covetousness, maliciousness; full of envy, murder, debate, deceit, malignity; whisperers, backbiters, haters of God, despiteful, proud, boasters, inventors of evil things, disobedient to parents, without understanding, covenantbreakers, without natural affection, implacable, unmerciful: who knowing the judgment of God, that they which commit such things are worthy of death, not only do the same, but have pleasure in them that do them.

Nathan can be safe if he keeps his eyes lowered, if he focuses on the plate of food that he can never taste. He lets the holy utterances fall over him like the lightness of a quiet rain, bows his head as if in reverence and listens, without hearing. In his mind he is far away, in the woods with Roy, stepping through golden sunlight.

Soon the meal will end and Dad will retreat into the living room, where the television will drone deep into the night. No one will expect Nathan to go there. He holds his breath and waits, watching Mom's knotted hands as they whiten on the handle of her fork. She closes her eyes, and for a moment it is clear that she too feels pain from this last scrap of their togetherness.

If Dad feels anything, he gives no evidence in voice or demeanor. He reads as if the words will take him back to the Dad of yesterday or the heaven of tomorrow. He eats. He sips whiskey. The daze of evening descends on him. When, one moment, he glances up at Nathan, he hardly seems to see anything at all.

He reads: *Wherefore God also gave them up to uncleanness through the lusts of their own hearts, to dishonor their own*

47

bodies between themselves; who changed the truth of God into a lie, and worshipped and served the creature more than the Creator, who is blessed forever. Amen.

The meal will end. Meals always do. Nathan will climb silently to his room again, to the peace and safety that has so far remained intact in this new house.

Chapter Five

In the morning Nathan wakens with apprehension, dressing with self-conscious care and eating breakfast slowly, almost as if he hopes Roy will leave without him. He is afraid the wrong Roy will appear today, afraid he will find the silent, cold one. But when he walks to the bus, Roy waits calmly. He says good morning before Nathan reaches the door, speaking with an openness that puts Nathan on guard. Nathan ascends while maintaining an invisible wall, longing to reach through it and touch Roy but taking his seat with a circumspect air. He studies the dewy yard beyond the bus window, the edge of the Kennicutt Woods.

As Roy closes the door and wrestles with the gearshift, he partially turns in the seat. "I almost came to see you last night."

"I wish you had." Nearly too low to hear.

"Me and my folks had to go to a business meeting at church."

"You go to church a lot, don't you?"

"My parents got a lot of religion." He has steered the bus onto the road, entering the stretch of forest. Once the houses have vanished, he stops the bus and stands. "Come here."

To hold him and be held by him is enough for Nathan. Roy says, "You better eat lunch with me today if you know what's good for you."

"I will." Into the cup of shoulder and neck. Lingering. Roy pulls him close, sighs.

"We have to go, I guess."

After that, the day is a fog, except for lunch when Nathan can find Roy and set himself into his orbit. As before, Nathan finds a table alone and, when Roy joins him, they talk before Randy and Burke arrive. Roy tells about his church, the Bethel Church of God in Congregation, which meets in a pretty white building on a nearby loop road. The preacher is a fat man with a bald spot on top of his head and hair all around it, and he preaches sermons filled with the hell of sinners and the damnation of souls. Pretty much everything you can do is wrong, Roy says, especially if it's fun. The description of the preacher, whose name is Rutherford Paschal, enlivens Roy as he gives it, and Nathan shares the vision, remarking innocently that he would like to see this fat bald preacher one Sunday. At this Roy's face closes shut, and Nathan understands that he has said a wrong thing. Roy remains silent until he leads Nathan to the smoking patio, where the sunlight, the calm of a cigarette and the voices of friends restore him. Nathan relaxes, but studies Roy nevertheless.

Wondering about Roy's church, about all the life of Roy that Nathan has yet to fathom. About the girlfriend, mentioned once and never forgotten.

Days pass and they are together often. Roy's chores suddenly require Nathan's presence, and Roy's homework begs Nathan's help. Some evenings they work at Nathan's house and some at Roy's. In this way, one night, Nathan meets Roy's parents, who are much older than Nathan's. The Connellys took a long time to have children, Roy being the only one of four to live past birth. Sometimes he visits his brothers and sisters in the cemetery near their church, he says. To Nathan, who is also an only child, it is curious to think of Roy visiting siblings in a cemetery. Roy's large, soft mother takes shots to control her blood sugar and nerve pills to help her sleep. The boys do their homework in Roy's bedroom, surrounded by Roy's baseball and hunting gear. But one night they work at the kitchen table as Roy's mother slices apples in the adjacent living room. Roy's father passes through on his way from the barn to the desk where he keeps the farm's accounts. There is a feeling of ill health about the mother and a taciturn, tough shell that protects the father, and they talk little. But there is also a feeling of peace and safety.

At the end of her apple peeling, Mrs. Connelly brings her white glass bowl into the kitchen and washes the apples again. She asks the boys if they have studied good, and they answer that they have. She asks Roy what he is learning in school and he tells her about advanced algebra and auto mechanics. She listens to the description of dismantled carburetors, fuel pumps, and polynomial equations, shaking her head at the complexity. "His daddy knows all about motors too, but I don't." She offers Nathan a fresh slice of apple. "And I never could do numbers. I don't think women have the minds for some things. I know a lot of people think that's old-fashioned, but I think that's the way God intended it."

"My mom doesn't know anything about motors either," Nathan offers.

"See there." She nods her head at the profundity of it all. "What about you, Nathan, what do you like in school?"

"I like to read science fiction books."

"You mean about space travel and all like that. Lord, I don't think I would like to have all that stuff in my head. I don't read too much, except the prayer magazine we get. *Guideposts*. I like that magazine. It's really a Baptist magazine, but I like it anyway. We're not Baptists, we're Holiness."

"We go to the Baptist church."

"With Preacher Roberts? I like him. I think he's handsome."

"You ought not to be talking about handsome men," Roy says, "you know Dad don't like it."

"Your daddy ain't studying who I talk about. And I do think he's handsome. Did you always go to the Baptist church, Nathan?"

"No, ma'am. My mom used to take me to the Holiness Church too. But my daddy didn't like it because they play electric guitars."

"No. You don't mean it."

Even Roy is interested in that. "Electric guitars in the church?"

"One time they had drums, too. You know, like in a band."

"Lord help me," says Mrs. Connelly. "I don't know about that. We don't do that in our church, we just have a piano."

"We've been Baptist since my daddy started going."

"Now I know you all moved here from somewhere."

"Smithfield."

"That's right. Your daddy told me. You lived in Smithfield."

"We didn't live there long. We lived in Goldsboro before that. And Tims Creek."

"I think Tims Creek is a nice little town."

"Don't you get tired of moving so much?" Roy asks.

Mrs. Connelly is watching. Nathan has the feeling they have talked about this before, and is therefore more guarded. "Sometimes. It's not so bad though. We lived in Rose Hill for a long time, when I was little."

Mother and son look at each other. Nathan becomes afraid they've heard something, a story about the reason Nathan's family moves from one place to the other. Something about why they left Rose Hill. Dad likes to move, all right, but never quite far enough.

The conversation ends when Roy's father comes from his office looking for a glass of tea. He waits pleasantly while Mrs. Connelly stirs her large body to put ice in a glass. They talk about the fall weather, the clover Roy and he are planting in the field next to the house, the abundance of fish in the pond. The ease with which the Connellys keep company with each other almost makes Nathan feel at home himself.

Later, they carry their books to Roy's room, which is smaller than it seems from the other side of the hedges, a narrow, angled space, mostly occupied by a bed and Roy's desk. High on the wall are shelves for his baseball trophies, a sturdy collection. Nathan examines each trophy scrupulously but makes no comment. Nathan studies everything with the same attention to detail, including the view to his own window. Roy leans beside him, then smiles. Finger to the lips, be quiet.

They study. Roy sits on his bed. In his own house he behaves less bravely and dares less than in Nathan's, and Nathan knows better than to get too close. He spreads his science textbook across his lap. He peers into the closet, through the shadowed crack in the door. He studies the poster of a famous baseball player. Roy murmurs aloud as he reads.

He and Roy take long walks, over the whole farm, till Nathan understands the scope of Roy's world. The sullen houses in the bare field become their landscape, and they wander around the pond, memorize the graveyard, visit the Indian mound, pick apples in the orchard, search out deer in the surrounding woods, hunt for foxes and squirrels with Roy's 22-gauge, or simply lie on beds of leaves with their shirts open and their hands ripening on each other's bare skin. Nathan learns that Roy will kiss but he will not kneel in front of Nathan as Nathan will kneel in front of him. Nathan learns that he himself is somehow different from Roy, governed by other laws.

Always the admonition is the same. *You can't say anything about this to anybody else. You can't do this with anybody else but me. Okay?* Followed by the cloud of guilt, the moment when Roy can no longer bring himself to look at Nathan or to touch him. The guilt clouds him worse each time.

One Friday afternoon, without warning, Roy asks Nathan, "Do you want to go riding around tonight?"

They are assembling their books on the school bus. Roy has headed down the metal steps, then pauses to ask the question. Turning almost casually.

Roy has always seen his girlfriend on Fridays. Nathan has never asked, but he knows.

"I need to ask my mom."

Roy shrugs.

Quickly, lest the offer be withdrawn. "I'm sure she'll say it's okay."

Roy shrugs again, but in a more friendly way.

"Come with me while I ask."

The request, unusual, reverberates. Roy considers, momentarily uncomfortable. A slow change takes place as Nathan watches; a new thought occurs to Roy and a smile spreads outward. "She'll like that, won't she?" he asks.

Crossing the yard, they are aware of each other, as if either of them could contain, for the moment, the consciousness of both. They are echoing in each other through the mown grass, they are feeling the freshness of air on Roy's shoulders, the brush of the rose bush against Nathan's sleeve; they are each feeling each. Into the door they walk, and Nathan's mom is in the kitchen as always, dark-eyed, sitting at the table reading a novel by Emily Loring. She closes the book with a dreamy sigh as the boys enter, and focuses on them with effort; and for a moment Nathan feels a tremor of chill. She is hardly in this kitchen at all, she has fled somewhere else, dreaming. But this blankness quickly passes. She returns to the room from Emily Loring's world and adjusts her eyeglasses across the bridge of her nose.

Nathan is preparing his request and nearly has the words in perfect order when Roy seizes the moment unexpectedly. "Please, ma'am, I was hoping you might let Nathan go out riding with me tonight."

"Well I knew you boys wanted something the way you busted in here like you did." Her expression is gentle and her focus on Nathan soft. "You want to go riding, son?"

"Yes, ma'am."

"You know your daddy don't like you to run around."

Nathan makes no response. But she smiles as if he has answered her with something pleasant. Brittleness pervades her voice and manner, the sense that she may suddenly say something more shrill. "Well, you never go anywhere except church, I know that's the truth." Brushing her face as if hair or insect touches her. "Your dad and me have a church supper tonight."

"I don't need to go this time, do I?"

She reflects. Glare on the glasses, momentary blindness. "I guess you don't. Him and me in church is plenty for one night."

"Thanks, Mom."

"You make sure you behave like you ought to. Your daddy is real nervous lately. You know how he is. I can't get him to lay down, he don't rest at night. He don't need any trouble from you."

This is her way of talking, as if Dad were a being of delicate sensibility, to be treasured and protected. But something else in her tone, some edge, awakens memory in Nathan. It is as if she is issuing a warning. But he tries to refuse the fear, he clings to his happiness, stubbornly, because he will spend the Friday night with Roy, the hours entirely their own. Mom looks at Nathan with the air of blindness returning. Roy stuffs his hands in his pockets as if suddenly shy. "Thanks, ma'am. We won't be out too late. I'll bring him back by eleven o'clock." Giving Nathan a secret within the look they traded. "Get ready and let's go. All right?"

"Yeah."

The screen door opens and wind rushes out. Suddenly Roy has vanished and Nathan waits to catch his breath in the kitchen.

"He sure seems like a nice boy." Mom adjusts her glasses and opens her book. "He's got a good way of acting. Don't you think so?"

"Yes, ma'am."

"You need any money?"

"I got five dollars."

"Well, that's good." She is white-eyed again, facing the window. "I like this house. I hope we don't have to move."

"Me too." Feeling suddenly fearful. "Are we?"

"Oh no. Oh no. We ought to be able to live here a long time. Your daddy likes his job. He likes Allis Chalmers, you know he always talked about working for them. I don't think he liked John Deere as much." She presses a curved fingernail into the jacket of the Emily Loring volume. "But he goes through cycles. You know. And he's real nervous, like, lately. You know. Because he's not making the sales."

Nathan knows. He is suddenly afraid. "He's not going to bother me, is he?"

But she is away. She is wherever she goes. "He's just got some problems on his mind. Don't worry."

He finds himself watching the loosening flesh at her throat, the place where the tendons stand out. A vein beats against the skin. She smiles without any comprehension. That is all. The sense of warning has almost vanished. Except, before she submerges into the yellowed pages, she murmurs, "Stay out of his way tonight." A chill touches Nathan along the spine. He watches his mother and her lost, empty face. He goes upstairs. She hardly notices he has gone.

He stands at the window until he sees Roy's shadow. Then a little calm nests in his stomach, and he can move.

Downstairs he says good-bye in a whirl of air and runs through the grass to the car, where Roy already waits.

But he is still strangled by the last moments with his mother, and he cannot explain to Roy why, for the first few moments, he has no voice at all. The car whips a train of dust along the drive, Roy steering with his arm propped in the open doorway. He glances at Nathan, who remains frozen in the sound of his mother's voice. "What's wrong?"

Nathan shakes his head.

"Tell me." The voice more emphatic, the arm no longer relaxed in the open frame.

Small-voiced. "I'm okay."

"You glad we're going out, aren't you?"

Nathan laughs, brushes the back of his hand against his eyes. He laughs again, watching Roy. Who shoves him roughly away, a gesture of play. "You're crazy," Roy says, and drives.

At the end of the dirt road, Roy turns in the unaccustomed direction, the highway toward Somersville.

"Where are we going?"

"To meet Burke and Randy at the railroad trestle." He relaxes against the open car window, driving one handed.

Nathan faces him in the seat. Delight fills him, leaving no room for any other feeling. Here is Roy, they are together in a car, it is a Friday night. This is like people do.

No mention of her, the unseen. No mention of where she is tonight.

The drive lengthens and they talk, as freshly as if for

the first time, more animated than ever. The confinement of the car encourages them in freedom with one another; and at the same time the privacy shelters them as neither forest nor graveyard ever has. They are alone in a protected place.

Roy talks about his father, about the farm, about his mom and her sicknesses, her problems with her heart, her sugar, the circulation in her feet. He describes his father's worry about her, and his worry about money to run the farm, and his silence about everything. He describes a life of cleanness, a father who wanted more sons, a mother who could bear only the one. He has aunts and uncles spread over the whole county and beyond, he has more cousins than he can name. He has lived on the farm all his life, and he thinks he could live there forever. He could be a farmer, he could drive the tractor and plow the fields till he's old and gray. Except he's pretty good at baseball and he might want to do that instead, play baseball in the minor leagues. He has no illusions about the major leagues, but the minors would be okay. When he talks about those things his voice rings pure as a bell, his eyes shining. He has a future, he can see it.

Nathan talks about the books he reads, about wanting a telescope, about the stars and planets of his imaginings. He talks about going to college if he can get a scholarship. Someday he would like to be a chemist. Or maybe an astronomer with his own telescope in an observatory up in the mountains, away from everybody, where the air is clear.

"You can't be away from everybody." Roy seems briefly troubled by the idea.

"Everybody but you," Nathan amends.

A shadow grows and fades across Roy's face. He wishes he did not wish. "That's good." Finally, though with a tautness to his voice. "You and me will be buddies even when we're real old. Don't you think so?"

"I hope so." Hoarse. Aware of the need to say only just enough.

They drive in momentary silence, afternoon sun fading beyond the car windows. One turn, then another, leads them further from home.

From behind the seat, sweating in a bag, Roy produces something startling, a cold poptop can. Roy opens the beer and Nathan watches guardedly. Roy tilts it to his mouth.

"You drink beer?"

"Yes." Roy eyes the road quietly, the noisy car slicing through the velvet cascade of forest. "You reckon you can keep quiet about it?"

Nathan flushed. "I don't care if you drink it. It's all right."

"Answer my question."

"Yes, I can keep quiet about it. I can keep quiet about anything."

Roy slows for another turn, jaw clenched. At the intersection of dirt road and asphalt, he studies, for a long moment, Nathan's face. "That's prob'ly a good thing." Setting the beer between his thighs, he lays his hand tenderly on Nathan's. The moment of touch passes quickly, but the aftermath blasts at Nathan like torches. Roy says, "We're going swimming. That's where we're going."

"But I can't swim."

"Then you can watch me."

The new road is mostly gravel. The sky darkens toward sunset, the heavy end of day settling over forest, automobile, and sky. Near a path where a car and truck are parked, Roy steers the car onto the soft shoulder.

They park beside the truck, bright blue, and walk down a road into the forest, nearly dusk. Mud ruts are dried and hard, and the road is almost overgrown, strewn with large branches tumbled from a summer of thunderstorms. Nathan keeps close to Roy's shadowed side. Roy says, "I tried to drive down here one time. Got stuck. Dad 'bout like to had a fit."

"Where are we?"

"Near the river. About halfway to Somersville. You can hear the water if you listen good and the crickets ain't singing too loud." He has brought the beer cradled in the bag in his arm, and swallows from the open can. "We go swimming at the railroad trestle down here. It's way high up off the water. That's where I'm taking you. We need to hurry before it gets too dark to swim."

They follow the almost-road to the railroad tracks, and then pick their way along the railroad ties. Late sunlight slants through thin pine trunks, spreading golden fire over the river. Nathan listens for any sign of the train, and Roy laughs at his expression. "It comes early in the morning and late at night. You can hear it a long way off. Don't worry. I won't let you get run over."

Ahead the trees divide and a spectral bridge rises between the banks, a stark metal framework carrying the train tracks across the Eleanor River. Distant laughter springs from the span, from the voices of unseen boys. Nathan recognizes them from the smoking patio at school, Burke and Randy, and something about the knowledge complicates the evening. Roy throws his arm over Nathan's shoulder with easy confidence, but removes it when the figures on the railroad trestle become more distinct.

Burke has begun to climb a metal ladder to the top of the trestle, a long way above the water. Roy scowls as Burke climbs, jaw muscles working. There is rivalry between Roy and Burke, Nathan realizes, slightly surprised. Burke reaches the top rung of ladder and swings over the rail, standing only a moment on the narrow steel ledge. Plunging forward, legs kicking, but silent. He hits the water with a dark splash.

"A boy drowned here last summer. Dived right into the river and never come up. They had to call in all these scuba divers to find him." Dead, tangled in some kind of weed growing from the river bottom, said Roy. While Burke, clearly visible, climbs from the riverbank in his dripping drawers.

Something about Burke's body makes Nathan embarrassed, almost ashamed. He finds himself watching Burke, who is rumored to be the strongest white boy in high school. His hard edges and crude thickness fascinate.

While at the same time Roy begins to undress, and Nathan watches him too. It is as if the fact that he knows he must conceal his interest in their bodies makes that interest all the greater, all the harder to hide.

Randy hoots at Roy. "Did you see that dive?" Indicating the laudable Burke, still getting his breath.

"Sure did." Roy swings over to the ladder and begins to climb to the top of the trestle. He has laid his shirt and jeans on the tracks. Hips sway from side to side as he climbs. Pale undershorts shine.

"What did you think about that?" Burke asked, water beaded on his shoulders.

He expects Nathan to answer. Nathan swallows. "It's pretty high."

Burke snorts. "It's high all right. I bet you won't do it."

"I bet I won't either."

For a portion of the trestle's passage over the river, the rails and ties run on a gravel embankment and gray gravel fills the spaces between the ties. Over the center of the span, however, the rail is supported on beams of steel, and between the cross ties is air. Nathan steps onto these cross ties, where Burke and Randy wait. The feeling of falling is already in Nathan's gut, as if he were plunging toward the river. He can see the dark river surface far below the ties. Trying to show as little of his fear as possible, he steps bravely, glancing down only at moments when he cannot control his panic.

"I'm with you, Nathan, I ain' jumping off the top part either," Randy says. His skin is colored like sand and freckles trace the curves of his nose and strong cheeks. Randy is plump, with a roll of white fat at his midsection. He towels Burke's back dry. "I got no need to break my neck."

"Well, I do," calls Roy from above, and Nathan stares upward dizzily, wishing for something to hold.

Roy steps forward into space, kicking his legs as if to keep his upright stance through the air; he falls into the river, fast as that. Surfacing, he flings water from his hair and laughs, looking up at Nathan.

At the same moment Burke steps toward Nathan and grips Nathan's shoulders in his hands. On Burke's face is a wicked grin, and at the center of his eyes is a blade of ice that frightens Nathan, even the first time he sees it. He grips Nathan's shoulders so tight they hurt. "Hey Nathan, we're glad you came out here to the river."

"Let him alone, Burke," Roy calls from the river. He has begun a slow swim to shore. "He can't swim."

"Well maybe he'll learn if I throw him in right now."

"Don't bother him, Burke. I mean it."

"I ain't bothering him. Am I, Nathan? Huh? Say something."

He shakes Nathan violently. The hands on Nathan's shoulders burn as Burke lifts Nathan from the trestle and suspends him over the water. Nathan fights panic, holds perfectly still in Burke's grip. Strong fingers gouge his arms. From the center of the trestle Randy stops moving and watches. Burke grins and shakes Nathan again, more gently. "Are you man enough to jump from here? Or do you want me to throw you?"

"I don't want you to throw me."

"Then you going to jump?"

Nathan holds perfectly still and looks Burke directly in the eye. The act of assertion calms him. He is strangely peaceful and feels no fear, even at the prospect of the fall. Something meets between them. He focuses on Burke's arms and shivering chest. Burke is big for his age, and his stomach is ridged and hairy. A feeling of harsh strength pours out of him, different from Roy. Nathan looks into this, into Burke's face, and says, "I want you to put me down."

Burke laughs and seems perplexed. Roy stands on the riverbank, watching. Burke releases Nathan. He backs away, leaving Nathan at the edge of the trestle. Nathan hovers unsteadily, glimpsing, below, his own face slipping beneath the dark water. As if the moment has divided, as if he has both fallen and not fallen. Shivering, he steps back to the center of the trestle.

Far toward the trees in the darkness Roy climbs up the riverbank to the neat line of cross ties. Everything dissolves into nightfall. Starlings are singing, and frogs on trees are smelling the dusk and croaking in choirs. Roy trots down the railroad track, stepping from tie to tie.

Burke meets him face to face. "I didn't throw him in the river. I should have."

"You better be glad you didn't."

"Oh hell, I'd have gone down and got him before he drownded."

Roy studies Nathan over Burke's shoulder. Nathan shakes his head emphatically.

Burke says, "That was a pretty nice dive, buddy."

"Yes, it was," Randy agrees. "You was pumping them legs."

"What did you think?" Roy asks Nathan.

"It looked like something was chasing you all the way down."

Roy laughs a little and Randy joins him.

The sun hangs low, soon to be swallowed by the line of trees at the horizon. Randy and Burke dive from the trestle again, the low part, and Roy and Nathan sit on the rail and watch them swim. A peaceful charge crosses the space between them, and they are aware of each other with special sight. Below, Burke is pretending to drown Randy, who pushes back with fury. The game goes too far and Randy nearly fights with Burke as they leave the river. But even this commotion fails to alter the stillness between Nathan and Roy. Roy says, "I like this place."

"I do too."

A soft splash echoes from someplace down river. The gray of dusk swarms. "I wish I could swim."

"I'll teach you. In the pond at home. It's easy."

Nathan accepts the proposition and secretly cherishes it. He says nothing more since Burke is running toward them, lumbering along the rail, sure-footed.

"I got some beer," Burke says, "you want to drink one?"

"I got some too." Roy reaches for his jeans.

"It's in the truck." Burke gestures. "You reckon we ought to go back?"

"I'm ready. I've had all the swimming I need."

Randy halts some distance from the center of the bridge. "I'm right thirsty too."

"You going to drink a beer?" Burke asks Nathan.

"He don't need to," Roy says.

"I know he don't need to. But I might ought to pour one down his throat just to see how he would act." Laughing with an edge of meanness.

They leave the bridge and find their way along the tracks as the sun eases behind the trees. Nathan feels as if he has been away from home forever already. Every moment echoes of Roy. They walk side by side up the tracks, steady presence, as Burke and Randy weave in and out.

Burke has beer in a bucket of ice in the back of his truck. He hands one to each of the others, also offering a can to Nathan, who shakes his head no, but with respect. They drink. Glimpses of the beer and hints of the acrid smell remind Nathan. When his father swallows liquor, his throat moves in the same snakelike motion, the undulating of long, smooth muscles. Nathan shakes his head, focuses on the moon in the fender of the truck, the sound of a river, the shadowy trestle, and the closeness of the three boys. The four. He can include himself. He stands near Roy as Roy swallows, his smile a little softened by the beer, and the curl of last evening light in the sky.

Burke has draped a flannel shirt loose over his shoulders. He is lacing heavy work boots over his ankles. He sips from the beer can like a suckling. Shadows obscure his eyes.

Randy dresses watching Burke's back. In Randy's eyes is a round blankness.

Roy drinks. "What are you boys up to the rest of the evening?"

"Riding." Randy buckles his belt and adjusts the silver buckle to get it properly centered. "We'll probably run around in Hoon Holler a little while."

"See if we can't get us some." Burke aims his voice into the grass. "You going out with Evelyn?"

Roy shifts uncomfortably. Nathan stares into space behind Burke's head. "No. We ain't going out tonight."

"She running around on you?"

"Hell no. We ain't going out tonight, that's all." His tone is meant to warn Burke off the subject.

Burke watches Nathan with cool deliberation. "She's a hell of a good girl. Evelyn."

This falls into silence. Nathan finds himself unable to look at Roy.

Finally Roy says, "We ought to go camping before it gets too cold."

"You reckon?" Randy inspects his countenance in the side mirror of Burke's truck. "Where you want to go?"

"Up toward Handle. You know where I mean? Past the Indian mound, up Old Poke's Road."

"My dad used to take me hunting toward Handle," Burke says. "It gets wild around in there."

"We ought to go," Roy says. Lightly touching Nathan on the shoulder, casual but inclusive. "That's where the haunted house is. Remember I told you?"

69

They sip beer and consider the proposition.

"You and Nathan ought to come up to Hoon Holler with us tonight." Burke is watching Nathan again, a direct inspection, almost a challenge.

"We might. We're going to ride around a little while too. We might see you around there later."

"All right."

The easy conversation continues through another beer. Randy and Roy talk about the deer-hunting season and baseball. They agree that baseball is a better game than football. Burke would be playing football except the team is mostly black and his dad won't let him play with blacks. The night rises full of sound, cities of crickets in one long ululation. Nathan watches the beer-changes in Roy's face, the slow relaxation of facial muscles, the heaviness of eyelids. Randy tells a story about a girl from Hoon Holler who is supposed to be pretty much of a whore, who will do it with anybody. Might as well stick your hand in a cow pussy as that, Burke says. And Roy agrees and they all laugh.

But the conversation excludes Nathan. What is curious is that the fact seems implicit in the circumstances, as if they all understand that Nathan will not participate, that Nathan has nothing to do with talk about a girl of easy virtue in Hoon Holler. He has only to add the smallest of laughs at the appropriate moment. He comes from another world than the one in which these boys live. He sometimes inhabits the same world as Roy, but right now it's hard to tell. There follows a round of talking about girls in mechanical ways, about how to slide your hands into a brassiere, or how many fingers a girl will let you put inside her thing. There is the round of talking about cars. Randy asks if Roy's dad still has that same John Deere tractor, and Roy says he bought a new Allis Chalmers.

So finally they all agree they might see each other later at the Holler. Burke cranks the truck and Randy climbs to the passenger side. Roy and Nathan watch them disappear down the road. Roy crushes his beer can in his hand, meticulously, till the flat ends are joined in a thin disk. He tosses the weight a long way into the woods.

"That was all right." Peering at Nathan. "Wished I had another one."

"I thought you had some more."

"Naw. I'm out." Roy leans on the car. Mumbling the words of some song, across the top of the car to Nathan. "I like to swim in that river. You'll like it too, when I teach you how."

"Is your girlfriend named Evelyn?"

Have the crickets ever sung so loud before? Roy seems to be asking this with his sudden astonished look of listening. Opening the car door, swinging it outward slowly, he says, "Yeah. I told you that."

The assertion dies in the air between them. Nathan eases himself into the passenger seat. Roy's weight settles into place behind the steering wheel.

"I was only asking."

"It's okay." Roy starts the car, looking straight ahead. The car rolls forward.

They follow the course of the river along the road, tall pines looming over them. Darkness drinks the headlights. Nathan finds it hard to talk, for the first time. Roy asks, "Are you okay?"

"I'm fine."

"You're not talking much."

"I'm just quiet. That's all."

"Are you having a good time?"

"Yes."

"You want to go somewhere now? You want to go to a movie? I don't mind."

But Roy drives instead, down Island Creek Road to Catfish Lake, then back to the millpond and along the quiet streets of Potter's Lake, then along another road behind Riggstown. Roy parks the car at the end of a dead-end fork. Abrupt silence when the motor dies. Trees press close on all sides. Roy sits tensely, gripping the steering wheel as if the car still moves. Nathan waits. Roy's knuckles whiten. He faces Nathan as if with much effort. "You mind?"

"What?"

"Coming out here."

Nathan slides across the car. He can smell Roy's sweetish breath. Their faces are close and their bodies aware of each other again.

"No, I don't mind."

"We can go to a movie sometime too." Where words were easy before, they suddenly come hard. Roy blushes and seems terribly confused. Nathan wonders if he is remembering the conversation about Evelyn. "I ain't trying to hurt anybody," Roy says.

"You don't hurt anybody."

Roy is searching for something now, and Nathan waits. Finally, in a jerky motion, Roy leans forward and kisses Nathan on the mouth. The kiss is wet and cool. A sweetness fills Nathan. Roy waits. Their cheeks are almost brushing. "Touch me," Roy says.

Nathan slides his hands around Roy's neck. Their hearts are pounding now, they can feel the acceleration. The choruses of night insects rise around the car, high-pitched, almost frantic.

Suddenly Nathan feels older than Roy, and from within him comes some force in answer to Roy's fear. He moves with surety, kissing Roy's face, reaching for Roy's shirt, making each motion easy and gentle, what he understands will answer Roy's need. Nathan leads Roy quietly in the car. The passenger cabin offers the most protection they have ever had.

It is a gamble. Nathan must never reach for too much, he has learned better. The trick is to gain access to the knowledge he has stored inside, without remembering how it got there. To move in a way he knows will please Roy without revealing the knowledge, which has a source. The motion of their bodies becomes a balancing act. They have abandoned most of their clothes and Roy is lost in the sensation of Nathan. Nathan has been kissing Roy's cock with his mouth but then rises over it and presses it against his buttocks. Roy groans in surprise as Nathan guides him

73

inside and they finish in violence, straining and sour. They lie quietly on the seat and Nathan feels the difference. Then Roy's confusion, his anger. Nathan comes back into his body. Roy watches him with a kind of horror and suspicion.

There is a deadly pause.

"Who taught you how to screw like that?"

Nathan tries to draw away, but Roy grips his arms. "Where did you learn? Answer me. Who have you been screwing like that?"

Nathan remains too stunned to answer and shakes his head. Roy takes deep breaths, a savage look in his eyes. His grip on Nathan's arm tightens. "Nobody taught me," Nathan says.

"You're lying."

"No, I'm not."

Roy raises his hand and Nathan flinches, cowers suddenly. Roy sees the hand and the recoil. He studies Nathan as if for the first time. As if he has never known Nathan before.

They dress in silence. Roy starts the car again, and they head for home. Nathan studies the stars through the window. The broken place inside him aches now. Roy will not speak to him because Roy thinks he is nasty. There can be no question of Roy's judgment. Amidst so much turmoil the other memories are hard to contain but Nathan manages well enough, until he remembers his mother's voice from the afternoon, *Stay out of your dad's way tonight.* A little fear seizes him and he reaches for Roy again, in his mind at least. Roy who feels, even now, like protection.

Near the farms again Nathan says, "Roy."

Roy shakes his head, refuses to speak.

"Roy. Please."

He parks the car in its usual place under the walnut tree. In the protection afforded by the tree shade they watch each other.

Something unexpected. Roy is crying.

From Nathan's house come sounds. A light on the back porch. The screen swings open, and a dark broad shadow waits there.

A silence like winter cools Nathan's gut.

Whether Roy is watching now hardly matters. Whether he understands, or ever will. Nathan says good night and gets out of the car. He heads across the dark yard toward the porch light and the shadow of his father, waiting.

Chapter Six

Nathan hurries past the bruising bulk of Dad, who watches him enter but says nothing. Mom is seated at the kitchen table with a cup of coffee in front of her but refuses to meet his eye. She says her tiniest good night, aiming her voice into the cup.

Nathan tries to round the table to climb the stairs. But Dad turns and faces him. His eyes are bloodshot and his puffy cheeks are shadowed with heavy beard. "Hey Nathan."

"Hey Dad."

"You don't want to speak to your dad, do you?"

"I said hey."

Dad steps toward him and he retreats, slides past Mom and to the stairs. Dad has frozen in place. Mom is raising the coffee cup.

"Good night," Nathan says.

"Good night," she answers.

"Good night, Dad."

He runs up the stairs. He tries to get his breath.

He says good night to the window across the hedges. He goes to bed with his clothes on in case he has to run. He lies in bed with blankets up to his chin.

He expects trouble falling asleep but dozes at once. He seems to sleep deeply for a long time, then wakes with a start. There is a light in the hallway. It is very late in the night.

From the hall outside the door a voice says, "Nathan." Nathan's heart stops, then pounds. Nausea washes through him. He lies perfectly still with his eyes closed. The shadow of his father falls through the door.

"Did you have a good time when you went out tonight, Nathan?" The sound of something sliding against the wall. The speech is slurred, but still distinct. "I'm talking to you, Nathan. I know you're awake. I saw your eyes come open. Did you have a good time tonight?"

Still silence.

"You better answer me or I'm coming in there."

"Yes, sir. I had a good time." Soft.

"Your mom was the one who said it was all right for you to go out. It wasn't me. I don't like it."

"Yes, sir."

If I close my eyes. If I do not see.

Again the sound of sliding. Something against the wall. Closer this time.

"Where did you boys go?"

"Swimming. At the river."

"Did you go swimming too?"

"No, sir."

"That's right. You don't know how."

A deep breath. The shadow moves. *If I close my eyes.*

"I'm glad you had a good time." Silence. Softness of air against the window. "Open your eyes. Nathan. Look at your Dad."

"I'm sleepy."

"Open your eyes."

Mom whispers from the stairs. Her voice contains a familiar high-pitched edge. Nathan remembers the sound, which he has not heard in this new house. "Harland. Harland. What are you doing up there?"

"I'm talking to Nathan." The sliding stops.

"Come to bed. Leave Nathan alone. He's tired."

"Let me check on Nathan. I'll be back down there in a little while."

"You promised me you wouldn't bother him." The note of hysteria rising.

"I told you it's all right. I'm checking on him to see if he had a good time." In the silence there is his coarseness of breathing, the sour smell of his body. Then retreating. "You shouldn't let him go out like that. He ought to come to church with us."

"He can go with us to church on Sunday. Come on downstairs."

Slowly, the sense of Dad's presence fades. When Nathan opens his eyes the room is empty.

Dream Boy

Beneath the blankets he shivers. Moonlight flows through the window. Nathan listens till the house is silent. He slips out of bed, creeping across the floor. Till morning he sits at the window, never closing his eyes.

Chapter Seven

As soon as the sun comes up, he hurries out of the house, stealing bread and a can of macaroni O's from the cupboard. He heads to the Kennicutt graveyard and sits there through the long Saturday, never moving beyond the silent graves.

His sense of time alters, and the day seems eternal. He has brought some of his schoolbooks and does homework in the morning, though in the chilly air he can only write for a certain length of time before he needs to warm his hands. From the high vantage of the cemetery he can see the whole shore of the pond, and he feels safe there at first. He holds his schoolbooks in his lap and scans the dark breadth of the pond. The world of Saturday morning, silent, unfurls.

Flocks of grackles descend like clouds coming down out of clouds, landing in the pecan orchard beyond the cemetery. The chorusing of their voices continues through the morning, an early flock, not much in a hurry, rooting through the leaves and branches for pecans that have fallen to the ground. The trees have begun to lose leaves, the green-draped branches of summer have thinned and are lifted lighter. Even later in the morning when the sun does a better job of warming things, even then there persists the hint of autumn deepening.

He reads about the geography of Argentina, how the gauchos ride the pampas green and wide. He reads the history of the building of the pyramids by uncountable thousands of slaves. He reads about a boy who tries out for a baseball team, finds a hidden talent for pitching, and leads his team to a state championship. This last book he borrowed from the school library because he wanted to learn something about baseball, back in the long ago when it seemed to matter that he learn more about things like that. He knows that this feeling pertains to Roy in some way but he does not examine the link too closely, he reads the book in a dreamy way through early afternoon.

The presence of Roy is strong in the graveyard. Nearby is the place of the cherub, where Roy and Nathan lay on the ground. A long time ago this happened. Even now, the memory makes Nathan feel safe. But all his thoughts move distantly, and he cannot sustain any feeling; he reads and pauses, he breathes and stares at the ground. When he reads, the boy in the story is Roy, and that makes the book, too, move distantly, images far in the background. Roy absents himself from the scene. As if he were a dream, now dissolving.

Once, in the afternoon, Nathan returns to the house, tiptoeing across the back porch and through the open

door. Mom lurks in the kitchen like a shadow. Dad's cigarette smoke curls in the motionless air, drifting from the
direction of the living room. The weight of his presence
drags Nathan as if toward orbit. Mom asks, silently, *Where
have you been? Will you come home?* Nathan eats the lunch
of soup and crackers, answers, silently, *I won't tell you
where I am because you might tell him*. The softness at the
center of her face houses her pain. But she accepts the
silence and turns away, and Nathan, hearing the heavy
footfall of his father, hurries to the yard again.

"Is that Nate?" Dad's voice echoes behind, but diminished. In the yard, where October is draining the leaves
from green to brown, Nathan sidles along the hedge, out
of sight of the windows.

Roy appears suddenly near the barn. He carries a pail
in each hand. His flannel shirt is buttoned to the neck, the
sleeves rolled to the elbow. He marches from the barn
door to the chicken house, boots crunching the gravel.
Nathan's heart beats fast at the sight. But Roy retreats into
the murk of the chicken house without a word. Stung,
Nathan hurries to the pond.

In the afternoon he tries to sleep for a while, making
a bed of the blanket and wrapping it around his shoulders. He has not thought far ahead. He stretches out on
the blanket and uses his schoolbooks for a pillow. Lying
in such a way that he can still survey the pond, he has
only to lift his head. He closes his eyes. Sounds follow, and
he jerks his eyes open and scans his part of the world.
One after another sounds intrude: a broken branch as if a

foot were stepping on it, the similarity of something to a cough, the shrill cry of a bird, or the wail of distant wildcat. His eyes come open for each sound no matter how tired or near sleep he is. He scans the edge of the pond for his father. He cannot feel safe.

Twilight finds him curled against a tree, hoping he will not get redbugs this late in the year. He has begun, dully, to consider how he will pass the night.

Night descends like a sharpened blade. Leaving the graves for the first time since afternoon, Nathan waits near the cluster of farm buildings. Early autumn brings a chill to the evening, and Nathan's thin shirt retains sparse heat. But the sensation of cold reaches him as if from far away. The facts of dusk surround him. Lights burn in the kitchens of his house and of Roy's. Roy's father ambles idly in the driveway, under western ranges of rose-stained clouds. Roy's mother hovers in the square of light over the kitchen sink, dismantling the remains of the family supper. The rolls of fat over her elbows shiver back and forth.

Later, Roy lopes out of the house and drives away in the truck. A baseball cap obscures his face.

Mom appears on Nathan's porch, wringing her hands anxiously in a dishtowel. She scans the distant fields. She is afraid to call for Nathan, because of Dad. But Nathan's supper is cooling minute by minute, and soon she opens the screen door and leans out. The plaintive sound flies across the farm. Nathan relents.

When he enters the kitchen, she moves without speaking to serve him food. Even the backs of her hands seem pale and drawn. She is cautious to meet his eye. Dad reads the Bible in the living room. His rhythmic mumbling cannot be mistaken. Now and then the sound stops, the page turns. Once, while Nathan eats, Dad steps into the doorway. The tug of his watching pulls fiercely, and Nathan shivers. Mother stands between the two, uncertain.

"Nathan is home," Dad says. "I'm glad." Then he returns to the living room with his back bowed. His mumbling ecstasy resumes. *Remember therefore how thou hast received and heard, and hold fast, and repent. If therefore thou shalt not watch, I will come on thee as a thief, and thou shalt not know what hour I will come upon thee.*

Nathan eats, hardly tasting. Mother turns her back.

After supper, Nathan steps onto the porch, studying the darkness that has settled over the world. The wind sharpens. Cold stars wheel in the sky. Nathan advances to the screen door, tests the air. The cold change of wind soaks him. He had thought about sleeping outside, but the chill of the wind decides the issue for him. He will face the house for the night.

In the kitchen he finds a ball of twine in his mother's drawer of odds and ends. Climbing softly upstairs, he takes a deep breath, bouncing the twine in his hand.

He ties one cord across the doorway, using the hinge and a low nail in the wall. He ties another cord from the bedpost to the same nail. About the height of a man's mid-calf. It is as if he has already prepared the plan. But even with the tripcord set, he will not dare the bed, which has been a trap in the past. He makes himself a pallet in the darkest corner of the room and sleeps there.

He adjusts to the hardness of the floor beneath the quilt. The odd perspective of the room requires study. The floor under the bed needs sweeping. Cobwebs under his desk catch light. He fluffs his pillow, closes his eyes.

It is difficult to keep his eyes closed. Like in the graveyard that afternoon, every sound jerks him awake again. Every creaking of the house is a footstep, every murmur of wood a voice. But he hardly slept the night before, and soon the need for rest overtakes him, even on the hard floor, even keeping watch.

At first, deep sleep. Then a new sense, a presence. At first the presence seems dreamy, unreal, and then there is a change. The surface of the dream becomes the room in which he sleeps. Nathan needs to take a deep breath but there is a weight on his chest. A sound, a door that creaks when it opens. He wakens to a crash as Dad, at some wee hour of morning, falls face forward into the room, feet bundled in twine. Dad cries in fear and rage. The sudden image reverberates, the shadow of the father falling, the loud slamming of his body onto floorboards, followed by harsh groans of surprise and pain. The image replays again and again as Nathan flees through the door, slipping down the stairs and nearly slamming into the white-gowned figure of Mother, emerging from her bedroom.

She asks something, but Nathan hurls himself through the house without answering. *Did he touch you?*

He bursts through the screen door into the wet grass. Burning stars herald the stranger part of morning. He runs along the hedge in the shadow. He sees the light in his own bedroom window. By the time the images clarify in his mind, he has passed the barn and runs, out of sight of both houses, toward the lake and the familiar path to the cemetery.

He finds his blanket and sits against the trunk of the water oak. He is shivering, his teeth chattering, he cannot get warm. He huddles with the quilt drawn up to his nose and his knees tucked under his chin, in the shadow of the tree with the view of the whole pond. For a while he thinks his father is searching for him but Nathan, patient, remains perfectly motionless. He can see the stars over the trees and notes the changes as the hours pass. Soon, whatever search was undertaken is abandoned. Nathan is alone, waiting.

At dawn he rouses with no awareness of having rested. Light rainbows along the horizon. Along the shore of the pond, heavy feet are walking. Distant, Dad clears his throat. The sound strikes Nathan with a cold hand. He remains motionless, partially sheltered by a tombstone. Feet are treading on dry leaves, in tangled grass. Across the pond Dad's dark figure flows along the water, walking with a bewildered slope to his shoulders.

For safety there is the whole width of the pond and the fact of black water. Dad's search already falters. He steps along the lake shore brushing aside low-hanging branches. Nathan flattens on the ground. Dad steps forward and stops. He studies the forest. He heads back to the house but stops again, straightens, as if he has taken a breath of youth. It's almost as if he knows where Nathan hides, as if by scent or sixth sense he can feel his son's presence across the water. For Nathan, the fear becomes vivid. But the cemetery neither beckons nor sways him. He stands like an intruder, the lowering shadows of branches across his face, his arms. His stance weakens, his back bends, he returns to the house. Where he will, no doubt, drink a little, then dress for church.

Chapter Eight

Nathan steps into the kitchen and closes the door.

The fact that the curtains have been drawn carefully across the windows changes the room. Something about the light reminds him of water, pools of water. There is even the sound of water, the faucet dripping, added to the almost inaudible murmuring of the television in the nearby room. But the house radiates a peace only possible when it is empty. This is Sunday morning, and Dad and Mom have gone to take their places on pews at the Piney Grove Baptist Church, Dad to nod, entranced, while Mr. John Roberts speaks the gospel.

Since he is alone, he dares to go to the room he usually avoids. In the living room the curtains have also been drawn, not quite closed all the way, and gashes of sunlight fall through, slanting across the couch, across the coffee table and the open family Bible. Dad has left the television to play for the empty room, volume low, pale images flickering.

In the bedroom that opens onto the kitchen, his parents' bed is neatly made. The remnants of perfume and aftershave mingle and drift. Mom has let open her round box of talcum powder on the dresser, and a brooch lies near it, reflecting a moment of light. The room comprises its shadows, surfaces, scents; nothing here can be touched. They have slept on the bed but all evidence has been concealed between the neatly squared chenille spread, the high fluffed pillows. He pictures them lying side by side on their backs, eyes closed, hands folded across their chests.

His own room lies exactly as he left it, pallet scattered in the corner. Mom has not even folded the blankets. Nathan finds extra socks and takes his coat. He steals— now he thinks of it as stealing—another quilt.

In the kitchen again, in the moment before leaving, he waits. The silence and stillness fill him with foreboding. For a moment, a thought of the future intrudes, a moment of *how long can I hide?* But he locks the door behind him and, hiding the key once again beneath the flowerpot, he escapes into the autumn morning.

A warm wind is rising from the south. Nathan should be in church, between the shadows of Father and Mother, beneath the massed clouds of Preacher Roberts's voice, in the presence of God. He finds that he misses the event. But he feels no need of a change in hiding place. Even for a second day, the cemetery seems safe enough. He remains among the dead Kennicutts and their married relations, sheltered from October wind by quilts and tombstones.

From there he can hear the cars return after church, can hear his mother calling his name, exactly twice, when Sunday dinner is ready. Discreet, as if Nathan has stepped into the yard to play.

Time slows to a crawl. He has finished all his assigned homework and finds himself idly reading ahead in the history text, penetrating the chapters on the Hittite, Babylonian, and Assyrian Empires. The history takes on the quality of fable or fairy tale, read outside time, among graves. The sun slowly arcs overhead.

Once during the afternoon Roy appears along the shore of the pond. His quiet ambling could hardly be called unusual, but something in his walk, in the carriage of his shoulders, broadcasts disquiet. He stops near the small dam on the opposite shore and seems to be watching the vicinity of the graveyard. Nathan, for his part, hides from Roy same as from Mom, same as from Dad. But when Roy's mother's voice summons him back to home, the sadness that descends on Nathan is all the more complete.

Lengthening shadows indicate it is the time of Sunday when Dad naps, a time that can be dangerous, when you can think you are safe, but are not. He is willing to forego the nap, if he is restless. He might be anywhere out there, searching, hidden in the woods on the other side of the pond. Dad might see any movement. Nathan holds so still every joint is stiff. As before, every sound becomes suspicious. The wild, tangled calls of birds rise in eerie echoes high in the tree tops from the deep forest that surrounds the farm. Nathan takes the blankets and books and searches out a more secluded place, behind a tree and a large stone grave marker, tilted at a wild angle but broad enough to hide him. He risks the movement even if Dad should be watching, his fear is suddenly so great. In the new hiding place, he is completely concealed.

But better concealment has its own price, that he himself can see nothing except banks of willows and slices of pond. He sits in silence, listening. Every possible footfall resounds. He is relieved when the sun sinks below the treetops, he is grateful for the cloak of shadow that descends over the graves. He can be less wary in the dark. He stretches, throws off the quilts.

With dusk he returns to the houses. The kitchens are lit and interiors shine. He slips through shadows, passing the ghostly windows of the parked school bus. He crosses the empty farmyard and slides through the gap in the hedge, into the yard where his mother can see him coming.

She steps to the screen door. Nathan stops at the bottom of the steps.

"I was worried sick." They stand there. They sense each other. A cough echoes from inside the house. "Do you want something to eat?"

Nathan studies her shoes. Tattered boat shoes, grayed with mud and detergent.

"He's watching the television," she says.

Inside the kitchen, Nathan sits with his back to the door. The smell and curl of cigarette smoke locate Dad where Mom has promised. No liquor tonight. He is apt not to drink on Sunday night if he is going to church. The absence changes the smell. Nathan breathes and listens.

Mom serves his supper silently. Dishes whisper onto the table. Silverware glides across plates, meat and vegetables appear. She could be serving spies. Dad, for his part, seems locked in an agreement not to hear. His coughs are regular, dry, almost weak. Nathan eats his supper, sitting like quarry in the kitchen, and Mom watches, mild-eyed and numb.

He eats, hands back the plate and stands.

"You can't go back outside."

Nathan runs water over his hands, dries them on a towel.

"It's going to be cold out there tonight."

He steps to the door. From the smoky horizon comes Dad's voice, "Who is that you're talking to?"

She freezes, also like the hunted. The recliner creaks when Dad rises, and the springs make a gasping sound when he stands. Nathan slips into darkness as the first of Dad's lumbering footsteps resounds.

By the time he reaches the shadows of Roy's side of the hedge, he can hear Dad's weight across the drying grass and fallen leaves. Acorns crack. Dad searches the yard abruptly, coughing his discomfort, never daring to call Nathan by name. The brute search halts as suddenly as it began. The screen door slams and Dad retreats.

Shivering. The night air has a biting edge. Nathan creeps further, to the border of the woods, not quite daring the graves as his shelter for the night. He retrieves his quilts but returns to the edge of the forest behind the houses, hiding himself in the underbrush. The houses remain clearly visible. The lights blaze from every window, Roy's included; only Nathan's own bedroom window is dark. He wraps himself in the quilts, as if in a cocoon.

The least sound rouses him to awareness; he is in a state between drowsing and wakefulness. He hears his parents drive to Sunday night service at church. Roy's parents do the same, and Roy is probably with them. The houses are dark, except for a dim blue bulb burning in Roy's kitchen, tracing the shoulder of the refrigerator in the frame of the window.

He is tempted to go inside, to sleep on a bed tonight, to take the chance. But he remembers the voice in the hallway, the crash of his father tripping across the twine trap and falling to the floor. He wraps the quilts tighter.

Both families return. Roy's church service ends the sooner, no surprise. Nathan's parents return late, when the waxing moon has risen. The house lights flicker on, ripple through rooms. They are flush from Christ's victory, they will read the Bible and pray in the living room. Mom will find no reason to change the routine tonight.

The night is cold again, and even two quilts are not enough to cut the wind. He takes shelter near a tree but it is as if the wind pours around it to soak him. He endures as long as he can. Later, maybe after midnight, when all the windows have gone dark in both houses, he sneaks into the school bus and curls up on a seat near the back.

For a while the cold and the smell of the seat keep him awake. The mundane interior takes on its own mystery in the half-light of the yard. But he has the quilts, at least, and some warmth accumulates beneath them. He sleeps for stretches, awaking and changing position, never quite comfortable, never quite warm. He dreams tangles of images from the last few days, boys diving through the air, a hand sliding along a wall, a voice in the hallway, a tangle of blankets in the corner of the bedroom. Then he wakens to the stillness and silence of the school bus.

Near dawn he sits and stretches, following his longest sleep of the night. The hard seat has given him a stiff neck and sore shoulder. He peers out the windows warily.

Light blazes across the yard, from the kitchens of each of the houses. The igniting of the lights must have wakened him. Mom stirs in the kitchen. She will be waiting for Nathan there, and Dad will still be sleeping.

So Nathan, rising and stretching, careful to remove the quilts from the bus, slips quietly across the yard and into his house again.

Mom allows him inside, looking once, deeply, into his eyes. She moves with the usual silence of morning, added to the other layers of her withdrawal. She is a blankness to her son. She has hardly slept herself. She is thawing orange juice into a plastic pitcher. He passes across her field of vision and creeps up the stairs.

His bedroom already seems a vacant, airy place. He chooses clean clothes. Washing his face at the sink, brushing his teeth, he feels a moment of normalcy. One more morning finds him getting ready for school. Except that his awareness is heightened. Dressing quickly, he listens for familiar footsteps on the stairs. He finds himself holding his breath, he hardly makes a sound.

So when he hears the customary sound of the bus motor warming in the yard, he welcomes the promise of escape.

He descends carefully, listening. Dad's snores wash the house in waves. Mom offers food and Nathan accepts a greasy slice of cheese toast on a folded paper towel. He carries this and his books into the yard, hearing, as a last low undertone, Mom's whispered good-bye. Nathan crosses the yard and climbs into the school bus, and Roy, gripping the steering wheel, sitting with a slouch, closes the doors.

Nathan hesitates, uncertain whether to claim his usual seat or whether to seek some refuge further back; finally Roy says, "Sit down," and Nathan sits. This action seals them even closer in spite of their inability to make the slightest sound. They listen. The bus hides them.

Roy drives away earlier than usual, then coasts slowly down the dirt road toward Potter's Lake. Once free of sight of the houses, Nathan breathes easily. He eats the bread and melted, now rubbery, cheese. The sense of peace fills him, as much for Roy's presence as for the food. As long as they are silent, Roy and he will be fine.

Still, he is a little let down when Roy stops the bus

and someone climbs aboard. But the noise and commotion are like steps descending into the day. He sits with his books in his lap, watching the back of Roy's head.

At the high school, Nathan hurries off the bus with the mass of kids, barely daring to nod good-bye. Roy concurrently makes a show of stacking his books.

For lunch, Nathan seeks out a new corner and keeps his back to the general congregation. He hardly dares wish that Roy would come, but, curiously, feels no surprise when he looks up and Roy is there. Roy ambles uncertainly with his tray before taking the facing seat. He glares at his plate like the first day. The wordless hinterland rises between them.

But he has come, whether they speak or not. The ritual of the cigarette also remains true to the past, the indolence of lounging on the patio beneath the swirls of smoke, Burke and Randy each handing Roy a free filter tip. They talk about swimming at the railroad trestle Friday afternoon, they relive the fantastic leaps of Burke and Roy. The memory of the day seems far away to Nathan. The wind over the cornfield, over the flat countryside, washing the patio, consumes him. The wind pours across the ground in rising waves. The flare of an acrid match in cupped palms sends smoke along Roy's cheeks. Cigarettes bravely burn.

After school, at the end of the ride home, Roy parks the orange bus in the yard, under the sycamore, and Nathan feels the heaviness of home.

They have been silent, the two boys, the whole afternoon ride. Safety can be found in spaces without words, where they are close together. Nathan is acute to some new change in Roy, some edge beyond his anger. The awareness has been building through the day and returns in force. Roy slides his books under his arms. He is delaying his departure. He affects to scan the floor with a critical eye. "I don't think I need to sweep."

Nathan dares no answer.

"There's some paper. But I can pick that up."

The distilled thread of television reaches them from one or the other of the houses. At the moment Roy and Nathan each seem alien to those clusters of rooms. But still there is some mistrust in Roy, some hidden resistance. They glance about. Nathan begins a step past the older boy. He can already feel the ground beneath his feet.

"Maybe you ought to come to my house tonight," Roy says.

Nathan hesitates, a split second. Too long to pretend he did not hear. "I don't think I can."

Because Roy is watching, Nathan has no choice but to head into the kitchen. He can feel Roy's eyes on his back the whole walk across the yard.

Mom freezes at the sink. Nathan softly closes the door. He says hello. After a moment she answers.

There is stillness. There is the monotone buzz of the Frigidaire. There is Mom's narrow back, the neat bow of her apron. There is the smell, antiseptic, of a freshly cleaned house. There is the neat kitchen, which lays itself out neatly in perpendiculars, squares, rectangles, diamonds. There is her voice, hardly audible, saying his supper will be ready soon. There is, pervasive, her fear, and its orbital chill permeates Nathan. There is also, suddenly, a past surrounding them both, resonant with the memories Nathan normally resists, the white spaces of time in which his Dad falls on him like snow. While Mother, adjacent, allows.

Now they cannot face each other, the mother and son. The rupture between them blossoms. Nathan heads upstairs, changes his clothes for the night. He is trembling for no reason.

He sits down to early supper in the kitchen, long before Dad comes home. She sets a plate before him, leaves the room. Her soft weight settles into a chair in the living room, followed by the whisper of Bible pages sliding across one another.

After supper he carries his plate to the sink. The sound alerts her to the end of his meal, but she remains out of sight, in that room where Nathan rarely ventures. For a moment, he wishes she would come and offer him something. Vague but comforting. He wishes she would come but she remains there. He eases out the back door into the night.

The house recedes. One by one his connections are falling away.

Tonight he does not even think about staying indoors. He carries his quilts out the back door brazenly. He wanders along the pond and by sunset he arrives in the Kennicutt graveyard with his coat and blankets. He sits at the base of the obelisk, the place where Roy first brought him, in sight of the stone angel with its chubby thighs. Listening to the wind, he warms himself under the quilts.

Tonight seems a little warmer than before. He sits quietly, the quilts heavy around his shoulders. He is more tired than he realizes and dozes suddenly, a burst of unconsciousness almost like an enchantment; and when he wakens, footsteps are crashing through the leaves and a shadow crosses his face.

In a panic, thinking Dad has found him, he rises, clutching the quilts. But the hands that take his shoulders are Roy's. Roy emerges out of darkness, they are facing each other. Uncomprehending, Roy. Looking Nathan up and down, astonished and then afraid. "How long have you been sitting out here?"

The decision to answer requires a moment of focus. "Since after supper."

Tree frogs are singing. The tenor of the birds has changed a little, the cries seem harsher tonight. The occasional cricket resounds. A mild October has yet to finish summer off. The two boys stand together in the sound of night. Warmth spreads through Nathan, and he can feel Roy's body yielding toward him.

They sit close on the blanket, without speaking. Their quiet draws them closer.

"You were out here last night too, weren't you?"

The memory is distant. "I got on the bus after a while."

They each reflect on the landscape. Roy asks no more questions. For a long time he cannot bring himself to look at Nathan at all, but Nathan waits.

Dad has been home a long time now. Nathan spots the dark shape of his car at its usual mooring. The cloud of his presence hangs over the house. But the fact of Roy makes the fact of Dad less fearsome, suddenly; Nathan contemplates the change with grave curiosity. He leans against Roy, who allows him closer.

They sit quietly for a long time. Finally Roy moves his mouth close to Nathan's ear. "I got to go inside pretty soon. My parents will be wondering where I am."

"It's okay. I'll be fine."

"You can't stay out here."

"Yes, I can."

Hesitation. Roy considers one question, refuses it, something helpless in his expression. "You should come to my house."

Nathan shakes his head. "Your parents will send me home."

Silence. Roy is wondering whether to ask what's wrong, Nathan can tell. But he rejects the notion, he is afraid to know. They stick to the practical.

"You can sleep in the barn tonight, I'll show you a place."

The voices of everything, of crickets and frogs and birds, collide with the rasp of wind through dry leaves in the trees overhead. Nathan trusts, and therefore neglects to argue. Roy pulls him close, like a brother.

They touch each other gently, without intent. Only once, when Nathan brushes his lips against Roy's throat, is there something else. Roy takes a sudden breath and grips Nathan's head with his hand. A moment of possession. And Nathan sees, in a fleeting way, the irony that what pleases him with Roy terrifies him with his father. He glimpses this, he has no words for the thought. The moment of dread soon passes.

Roy takes him to the barn through the back and shows him the mattress in the corner behind bales of hay. They cover it with yellowed newspaper and Nathan curls up in the quilts. Roy lingers a little while, till Nathan's eyes adjust to the light in the drafty structure. Light from the yard pours through chinks in the outer wall. An owl is hooting somewhere overhead. Roy leans over Nathan on the mattress, hesitant. The moment begins intimately but ends awkwardly, Roy decides against any touch, stands and wipes the back of his jeans. "You'll be safe in here. Okay? I have to go."

"Thanks." Studying the play of shadow on Roy's face. "Are you still mad at me?"

The question surprises Roy. For a moment he seems overwhelmed, though the question is very simple. "No, I'm not mad."

"I had fun the other night."

"So did I."

Nathan busies himself spreading the quilts.

When Roy heads to his house, the open door floods the barn with light. He waits in the rectangle a moment, his long shadow bisecting the stream of light. But whatever weighs on his mind, he asks nothing.

The door swings closed and Nathan is alone. The barn seems larger now that it is all dark again. The quiet and stillness are welcome. Nathan lies back along the mattress, newspaper rustling. He inhales the aroma of old straw, the dusky undertones of dried manure, a whiff of rotted apple, other odors he cannot identify. Around him, shadow-shapes are forming in the dim light that spills through the cracks in the walls; the stored farm equipment, the tractor and covered plows, protective, like sleeping giants. He studies the unfamiliar space and tries to make himself comfortable on the mattress, grateful that he is inside for the night. Tired after two nights of fitful rest, he sleeps more soundly than he would have thought possible.

In the morning, he wakens to the sight of Roy, who sits on the edge of the mattress. Nathan did not even hear the door open. "Good morning. Did you sleep?"

Nathan rubs his eyes. "Yes."

"Your mom is awake. The light's on in your kitchen."

Nathan stretches, sits up. "What time is it?"

"Early." Roy thumps his shoulder affectionately. Indicating the quilts, he says, "I'll hide these. You go get ready for school. Okay?"

When Nathan rises, Roy brushes close to him, kisses his cheek. Then Roy busies himself getting feed for the chickens. Nathan hurries to his house, leaving the barn by the back.

A cold, clear morning greets him. Nothing much has changed inside the rooms; his mother hardly speaks to him, his father lurks out of sight. His room lies exactly as he left it. He rushes to spend as little time as possible there, washing off at the sink, throwing on clothes, gathering schoolbooks.

So his life settles into a kind of twisted routine, and for the rest of the week he hides in the graveyard and sleeps in the barn, with Roy's sanction. After school he does his homework as quickly as he can, sometimes daring to work at his desk, in his room, or sometimes studying outside in the last of daylight, in the graveyard by the pond. Mom readies his supper early, before Dad comes home, and when she calls, he enters and eats quickly. The food is set out on the table as if by chance, Mom never stays. As soon as he has eaten, he retreats outside again, to spend the early evening hours in the graveyard or near the pond. Roy keeps him company then, if his own chores are finished, if they are not going to church, and if he can get away from his parents.

Nathan becomes a visitor to his former life, moving like a stranger in his own house, gliding through the kitchen, slipping quickly through doorways and along stairs. At his appearance, Mom retreats into other rooms. It is as if, as long as she does not see him, she can pretend that everything is fine, that he is still living in the house, that he is simply out of sight. The whispered sounds of her various habits, needlepoint and Bible reading, are the only signs of her presence.

Even when he sees her, early in the morning when he slides into the kitchen, she remains somewhere out of reach. Across her face drift strange, sudden expressions: fury, heartache, confusion, fury again, then quiet despair. Her whispered good mornings fade by Wednesday to the merest nod of the head. Nathan moves cautiously when he is near her, as if they have become animals circling each other.

She never asks where he shelters himself at night. She never asks how he stays warm, where he sleeps. She pretends. Never once, during the whole week, does she neaten his bedroom, make the bed or fold the blankets in the corner. They lie as he left them, the night Dad tripped over the cord and Nathan fled. Time stopped. The room has become a haunted place.

On Thursday, when he has dressed for school and is headed out of the kitchen for the school bus, into the kitchen Dad suddenly lumbers, terrifying and large. He shambles toward the refrigerator in white underwear, his blue-pocked belly overhanging the elastic, his craggy chest shivered with goose flesh. Nathan stops breathing, caught in the doorway. Dad smiles. The kitchen echoes with his cough. He ogles Nathan up and down and his eyes, red-rimmed, fill with longing. He steps toward Nathan without warning and Nathan backs up, a corner catches him and all at once there is no world, there is only Dad's white belly shivering with blood and Dad's breath blowing down from above, the shadow falling over Nathan's face. Nathan's heart batters his ribs. A sound falters. Mom's voice emerges from the other room and her footsteps cause Dad to turn. "Who's in the kitchen, Nathan?"

She stands in the doorway to see. Her flesh has gone gray. She is staring at her husband as if he has stepped onto the linoleum from another world.

Nathan slips free of the corner and hurtles out of the house; breathless, he reaches the bus at a dead run. Pushing open the cold metal door, he huddles in the chilled interior till Roy finds him.

"Is anything wrong?" Roy asks, seeing his stricken face. But there are no words, no words will come. Roy, so close to his own parents and his own real life, does not even dare embrace him. He studies the light in Nathan's kitchen, a long time, before settling into the driver's seat.

Puzzled, mostly silent, Roy has remained a steady guardian. Each morning he has come to the barn early, to wake Nathan when he starts his chores. He warms the bus ahead of schedule and watches the back door of Nathan's house. He acts as if this is the most natural change of habit in the world, and they drive away. During school they keep to their usual pattern, eating lunch together, then hanging out on the smoking patio with Burke and Randy. At night they wander in the woods, along the edge of the pond and among the slanted shadows of tombstones. They never discuss what has happened. Roy never asks, and Nathan never volunteers.

They talk with their bodies. Roy says he is sorry again and again and never makes a sound. In the woods, in the shadow of the tombstone of Sarah Jane Kennicutt, on the path to the Indian mound; never in the barn, for fear someone will hear. Never near the houses. They hold each other on the borders of the farm, at the edge of wild country, they speak with their hands.

Sometimes when Roy watches, a question can be read in his eyes. Who is Nathan, why is Roy with him? Nathan can almost hear the words. Who is Nathan?

Roy goes away with his family to Wednesday night prayer meeting. Evelyn will be there. Nathan pictures her as blond and tall, with a sweet face, plump, round breasts and full, wide hips. She is waiting for Roy at the door to the sanctuary. She is holding a bouquet of flowers in her hand.

The late nights are the hardest times, after Roy says good-bye and closes the barn door. The smells, the unfamiliar shadows and sounds, trouble Nathan's sleep. The dirtiness of the mattress and the dust of the straw beside it make him cough, and at times he becomes afraid Dad will hear him. He wonders, when he will allow himself to think of it, how long he can go on hiding.

On Friday, while they are lounging on the smoking patio, Roy lets Nathan taste his bitter cigarette. He inhales sharply, the hot smoke searing his lungs. The choking and coughing that follow bring general laughter, and Burke and Randy clap Nathan on the back. There follows a moment of such sheer friendliness that Nathan loses his fear of Randy and even of Burke. When Nathan catches his breath they are talking about camping, about the trip to Handle they discussed when they were diving off the railroad trestle, Roy, Burke, and Randy. Roy is including

Nathan in the plans for the trip, and Nathan realizes with relief that this could solve the problem of how to get through the weekend.

Near the end of the day, Nathan finds Roy waiting outside Advanced Math. The surprise of his appearance helps Nathan to see him fresh and vivid once again, tall and strongly made in his jeans and denim jacket, the high bones of his face darkened with a trace of beard, his lips cut in a lopsided smile. Fierce eyes shock from beneath dark thick brows. Roy falls in silently beside Nathan and they head under the canopy to another class. "You think it's a good idea to go camping this weekend? If you're worried about your mom, I can ask her for you."

Nathan remembers the sliding shadow in her housecoat, the deepening dark circles under her eyes. "It'll be okay. She'll let me go."

They have arrived at Nathan's final class. Roy has led the way, and at the last moment lays his hand on Nathan's shoulder. The almost hidden gesture passes unnoticed in the general commotion of classes changing, but for Nathan the brief nervous flare sears him. "I'll see you after school."

Roy hurries to his own class. Nathan takes his seat in Biology, opening his text to the chapter on cell mitochondria.

The bus ride home is intimate in a way Nathan can hardly credit, as if, out of all the noisy creatures on the bus, only he and Roy truly exist. Even when Nathan looks out the window at the tattered autumn fields, Roy watches from the overhead mirror, eyes hanging in the air.

He stops the bus on the dirt road, when all the others

have gone. He calls Nathan to the front of the bus. The press of his body is familiar and heady. He traps Nathan's head against his chest. They hold still against each other, breathless through silence, till the distant drone of a truck motor warns them of itself. Roy releases Nathan unhurriedly. "We won't have to worry about this kind of shit in the woods."

Still without hurry, he reclaims the driver's seat and they finish the drive home, sliding into the parking place beneath laced branches.

Nathan gathers his books. When he stands, so does Roy. They walk together to Nathan's house.

In the kitchen, Mom faces Roy with hardly a trace of surprise. Roy stands straight, brushes back his hair, asking his question in a manner that manages to be both courteous and bold. He says he wants to take Nathan camping for the weekend, till late Sunday, and he's sorry not to have asked sooner but him and his friends just thought of the trip and this is the perfect weekend for it, almost the last one, really. The weatherman says it's going to be warm and pretty, like a little taste of summer. He says he'll look after Nathan and nothing will happen to him. She laughs nervously when he finally stops talking. "Nathan doesn't even have a sleeping bag."

"I have an extra one."

He faces her with calm assurance. Something about his directness makes her shy away, as from a too-bright lamp, and she turns aside. "Yes, I guess it's a good idea."

"Pardon me, ma'am?"

"I said I guess it's all right. He can go." She nods her head toward Nathan without looking at him.

Roy comes upstairs with Nathan to pack, counting what he should bring on his fingers. The fact that Nathan's dad could come home any time adds urgency, and they move quickly. Nathan owns no backpack so he gathers clothes and necessities in a bundle for packing at Roy's house.

Roy explains the camping trip to his mother with an air of presumption. Nathan and he are to meet Burke and Randy at the Indian mound as soon as possible so maybe they can hike farther into the woods before sunset. This means you need to hurry, Roy says, moving deliberately from one task to the next. He sets his mother to packing provisions, and she slices bacon and cheese and wraps slices of bread in plastic. Roy gives Nathan clear, concise instructions on counting tent pegs, bundling them properly, tightening their shared canteen so it does not leak, fastening the snap over the head of the knife to keep it sheathed. He checks everything and finally divides the bundle into two packs. Nathan's is lighter but the weight is still substantial, and the fact pleases Nathan in an odd way. He walks easily even with the weight on his back. He feels suddenly sturdy, as if he could carry the pack forever, and walk forever, into the woods.

Roy's mother stands in the yard to wave them off. Nathan's mother is nowhere to be seen.

Chapter Nine

It is easy for Nathan to refuse to look back. He has been granted two days of safety, and the woodland enfolds him in green gold. By now the pond and cemetery are familiar landmarks, and Nathan knows by certain signs—the particular twist of a branch, the bend of the creek that runs through the woods here—that they are following the path to the Indian mound. Roy's long strides set an easy pace and his silence engulfs Nathan so that both move with attention to quiet. The country thereabouts is haunted with memories of the courtship between the boys, and near the creekbed they look at each other. "Don't say anything about that," Roy warns, but he is laughing when he says it.

On the Indian mound they see two figures waiting. Burke and Randy hoist their backpacks, moving in tandem. Burke hollers, "About time you lazy assholes got here," and Roy answers, "I get where I'm going exactly when I please," as he and Nathan climb the mound.

A shyness overtakes Nathan during the climb, and he

is almost speechless when Randy claps him on the back. "I see you got your ma to let you come with us. That's good, I'm glad."

Burke spits into a patch of golden leaves, saliva stretching to a thread. "Nathan ain't no baby."

Wind sends a shower of maple leaves around them. The sharp chill of approaching dusk wakens Nathan to his freedom. Randy asks where they're going, and Roy answers, with an air of mystery that restores his swagger, that it's a secret place his uncle showed him, a good long walk into the woods, pretty far from everything. Up toward Handle, a direction the others seem to know. Burke and Randy ask more questions but Roy refuses answers. They will have to wait and see.

So Roy sets out walking east and everyone follows. The sun hangs high enough that the forest is full of light; and the peaceful afternoon expands. For Nathan it is as if he has walked out of Friday into some ceaseless stillness, a timelessness of superior quality. The shadow of Dad vanishes. They march through bright-colored splendors, high leafy vaults, waves of vine and frond. The red and silver maples have turned colors, but the oaks and pines are still retaining their green. The images of the other boys shimmer against the fervid backdrop. Burke's bronze arms slide among the leaves, his dense body careens through the dusk, heavier than its surroundings; Randy's rounder figure follows in Burke's wake, his golden hair sometimes disappearing behind Burke's back. Nathan occasionally turns back to study the two, but mostly watches Roy's smooth gait, the movement of his shoulders beneath the backpack, the gloss of dusk in his jet hair. Nathan trails him like a lesser moon.

It is a kind of church, requiring reverence. This revelation comes to Nathan as he is gazing from side to side, guarding the delight and freedom of the moment as if they must be protected carefully in order to preserve them. He refuses to allow happiness to show in his expression, cultivating the careful indifference of Roy, the swagger of his hips, the practiced ease through-and-under branches. They are swimming through golden light, traveling through a green- and gold-leafed choir.

Down a drastic slope of hillside strewn with uprooted trees flows a creek through a dark cut of land, the creek swathed in Joe-Pye and cinnamon fern, overhung with shreds of Spanish moss. Along the flow of creek Roy leads them, where the moss is lush and the ground soft for walking. Nathan is careful of his silence here, where fallen branches threaten to break with a snap, where dry leaves crackle like bones. He has lost any sense of time, they might have walked for leagues. Only birdcalls and the caucusing of insects can be heard. Sunset threatens before they halt for the night, and Roy has really pushed them too far, as if to put distance between them and the farm. They scramble to set up camp before dark.

Roy builds a cook fire, digging a shallow pit and ringing it with stones. The fire burns like a golden shrub. A thin thread of smoke wraps round and round itself and climbs. Warmth creeps up Nathan's arm. Roy grins. "You look happy."

Nathan nods in a small motion. "I like the fire."

"Me too."

Burke and Randy have set their own tent near a shower of red maple, a splayed branch like an overhanging mist; they move awkwardly with bent elbows, scowling as they unpack for the evening. The dark creek flows past, and blood-colored leaves corkscrew slowly toward the sea.

The woods are nearly dark but for the circle of the fire. When preparations for supper bring Randy within the perimeter, in the dregs of daylight Nathan searches out a path to the creek and stands at the edge, his reflection shimmering in the glassy surface. The songs of night birds have begun, added to the throb of crickets, the pulsing of tree frogs, the nearly human sobbing of a wildcat. Soon smells of frying bacon travel from the campfire, where Randy and Roy have begun cooking, a scene like alchemy, the two figures lost in swirling smoke and spark showers. As if he feels Nathan's watching like a touch, Roy raises his head directly to Nathan across the glade. Their shared smile is a secret only they can see. The space between them has grown strong, suddenly. A room in which they are always walking.

The supper of small talk passes, bacon wrapped in white bread, water from the creek, cheese. Nathan washes the dishes afterward, kneeling by the creekbed. Neither stars nor moon can be seen tonight; dark clouds are rolling overhead. The pitch of insect and frog song rises, then the wind picks up the note and outsings everything. Gusts whip the campfire and towers of sparks rise briefly over the heads of the boys. They are listening to the forest, no one is speaking. Smoke from the fire flies toward the murky branches, vanishing within the tangles. Tonight the world is wide and has a clean, sharp smell; the feeling of open space overwhelms Nathan and he flares his nostrils at the change of air, the taste of lightning. Roy stands with his hands in his pockets and his head thrown back, drinking the world through closed lids. He is breathing with a strong, steady beat. "I'm glad we came out here," he says, to no one in particular, and Burke grunts at him and Randy echoes his words.

Burke pulls out a little bottle and passes it around. Roy sips from it, and so does Randy. Nathan sniffs the whiskey and passes it back to Burke, who sneers. "Don't want none for yourself?"

"No."

"What's the matter?"

"Nothing's the matter."

Burke swallows, then caps the bottle. He stares at Roy, at Roy's face in the fire. "You want some more?"

"Not right now."

Burke shrugs. "Just say when, podner."

"It's been a lot of people killed out in these woods." Roy smiles at Nathan, across the fire.

"Don't start this shit, Roy." Randy takes the bottle from Burke.

Burke laughs.

"I mean it. It was two men killed out here this summer, wad'n it?" Roy nods to Burke.

"That's right. Two of them."

"Them two suckers from Blue Springs. They found one of them hanging upside down with his nuts cut off. You 'member, Burke?"

"You're full of shit," Randy says, "there wad'n anything cut off of them."

"That's not what the deputy sheriff told my dad. They found one of them men hanging upside down, and his nuts had been sliced off at the root, and his eyes popped open from hanging upside down like that, and he bled to death. They still don't know who done it."

"And they never found his nuts, neither," Burke hooted, laughing.

"Nope, they never did."

"You two sonofabitches better shut this shit up."

The gale of laughter at Randy's expense precedes silence, and the bottle goes round again. Roy drinks. "There was one man who was killed out here one time, they chopped his head up with a hatchet, so bad you couldn't even tell who he was, and my dad used to see him sometimes in our back fields, still walking around like he was looking for something. He would come right to the edge of the woods and look out, and that was all he would do. Then he would go back and look somewheres else."

Randy refuses to respond. Arms crossed, he stares upward into the shadows of branches.

"You know a lot of stories like that," Burke says.

Roy takes this as praise, pleased with himself. "What do you say, Randy? You want to hear some more ghost stories?"

"Suit yourself." Tight-lipped.

"Tell that one about the bloody red hand," Burke says, "that's the one I like, you know, with the mansion, and the knocking at the window, and all."

Roy sips from the flask again, and stirs up the fire. Leaning back on his arms, he studies the fire and recites his story, about the man in Somersville who killed his girlfriend's husband and chopped off his hand, only to be pursued thereafter for the remainder of his days by a Bloody Red Hand, which could enter through the window of even the most secure chamber, after knocking on the window three times first, and then entering and creeping across the windowsill and strangling its victims with bloody red fingers. Killing the killer's most precious relations one at a time before finding the killer himself at last. "And the police have that whole story right down in their files in Somersville, only if you ask them about it, they act like it never happened."

He tells the story of the Devil's Stamping Ground, a place in the woods where the Devil comes to dance, you can see his hoofprints baked into the ground, and if you sleep too close to the circle, you're never seen again.

Then he told the story about the time a driver

stopped to pick up a hitchhiker near Goldsboro, and she told him who she was and said she was on her way back home from a dance when her boyfriend had car trouble. And her name was Sweet Sue and she seemed a little dazed, like something had happened to her, like maybe her date really dumped her on the side of the road, and so the driver took her home, to this address she gave him in Goldsboro. And when the driver parked the car and went around to help her out, she wasn't there. So he went and knocked on the door of the house, and he told the story of what had happened to this old woman who came to the door, wrapped up in her housecoat. And she told him that she once had a daughter named Sue, and she died in a car accident twenty years ago, on the night of her high school prom. And now and then somebody like the driver would stop at their door and tell the story of how Sue was still trying to get somebody to bring her home, after all that time. "And I know that's a true story for a fact, because my Uncle Heben lived next door to them people, and he was there sometimes when people would try to bring their daughter home."

In the end, Randy listens like the others, and they pass the bottle back and forth while Roy tells every ghost story he knows. Till the wind redoubles, and Nathan glimpses the movement beyond the highest branches, the roiling of cloud bottoms across heaven.

"Listen to that," Randy says.

"Storm coming up." Roy points to the south. "Wind changed right after supper. Did you feel it?"

"You mean it's going to rain?" Randy asks.

"Yep."

Burke says, "Fuck."

"My tent is dry, and I got it on high ground for the night. I don't know about you."

Burke glares at Roy for a moment. Then, silent, he lurches up from the ground and slouches off to check.

A moment later his deep voice booms for Randy, and they move their tent to a better vantage. Roy and Nathan follow to help.

The coursing air is a continual singing now, and the hollow sound sends a chill through Nathan. They move the tent quickly and Nathan soon finds himself at the creek again, staring into the darkness and listening. The keen fresh scent of the storm sweeps over the forest, over the boys and their small tents. The tattered fire is blowing in the rocks, bravely sustaining.

From behind, Roy says, "I hope you see something in that creek, you stare at it enough." His tone is joking, but there is a serious shade.

"I was listening to the storm come up, I wasn't really looking at anything."

Momentary nearness allows the heat of his shoulder to cross to Nathan's. They watch each other sidewise, they inhale. Wind drowns out thought and speech at once. A crashing. "Listen to that. Wild."

"It sounds like somebody's voice," Nathan says. "I can almost hear words."

They watch each other. Roy smiles. He almost reaches,

almost embraces. But at the last moment his face clouds and the smile softens.

A drop of rain crashes against Nathan's forehead, another on his shoulder, and around them leaves are shuddering with the impact. Roy is watching Nathan fervently. "You aren't scared out here, are you?"

"No."

But Roy goes on watching, and Nathan blushes.

Voices summon them from the campfire. Burke and Randy are waiting, Roy and Nathan return, as the fall of rain builds to steady percussion. "Listen to that wind," Burke says. "It sounds like some girl crying her eyes out."

"It sounds like your girlfriend crying because she has to stay home tonight," Randy says.

The phrase pleases Burke visibly. "Hey Roy, what's Evelyn doing tonight? Is she sitting home? Or did she find somebody else to take her out?"

Roy studies his hands, attempting to control his expression. "She's home with her parents where she belongs."

"You sure about that?"

"Ain't none of your business what I'm sure about." Brow darkening, he watches Burke with a warning expression. Scattering rain has begun to flatten his dark curls.

Burke grins and gives Nathan a wink. "I guess I heard that."

"This rain sucks," Randy says, eyeing the upper tiers of forest, where the air is filling with a gray wash. His voice disperses the sudden tension. "I sure wanted to sit around this fire for a while."

"Well you can sit around some wet rocks if you want to, but that ain't going to be a fire but another minute or two." Roy eyes the hissing of water drops in the bright embers. "I'm about ready to crawl in that tent. I'll see you guys in the morning."

Signaling Nathan with a glance, Roy heads to his tent. Randy has turned to do the same, leaving Burke alone in the clearing, rain plastering his shirt to his skin; he watches the fire with strange ferocity. Nathan follows Roy but turns at the last moment, as if summoned to do so. Burke is staring at Roy, his outline blurred by rain. From a pocket Burke pulls the narrow bottle a last time, uncaps it, drinks, licks his lips and pockets the bottle again. Still watching Roy. Nathan hurries forward.

Roy waits at the edge of the thicket, with rain scattering on the low underbrush and draining through the carpet of pine needles. Vague light encases him in a kind of cloud. He welcomes Nathan onto the high ground, into the trees; the rain swells in the air and both boys are wet when they crawl into the tent. Nathan can feel Roy breathing. They kneel, side by side, in the canvas darkness, with the mansion of dusk and rain collapsing around them.

They dry themselves with towels. Roy lies along his sleeping blanket, resting his head in the crook of his arm. Nathan hovers, they wait. Roy reaches for Nathan, pulls him down.

The scattering of rain becomes a rhythm, and their breathings merge with the easy, syncopated sound. Nathan closes his eyes, pretends the tent is a cave, pretends they are in a time a thousand years ago, or farther, they have traveled into prehistory, they are alone in the world. Roy's face is like a light in the darkness, luminous from within like flowers at dusk, and when he exhales he voices the slightest note of music. His moist breath runs down the nape of Nathan's neck, curling along the delicate spine. Peace runs through Nathan like currents of water, his body throbs with safety, and they seem so joined in that moment that Nathan can feel the pulse of happiness in Roy as well.

When Roy finally stirs, it is to release a fuller sound, a long, easy, expanding sigh.

"Thank you for bringing me out here," Nathan says.

He is uneasy and silent for a moment, as the rain throbs along the canvas and the wind continues its strong insistence, its pleading through the leaves. "I used to go camping with my dad when I was little. We don't do much stuff like that anymore."

"My dad and I never did stuff like this." The sentence breaks a little. Roy draws him closer.

"I don't like your dad much." In the tent Roy's face is hard to read. But there is a stillness to his voice. "He came out to the barn yesterday. To talk to me." Shy suddenly. From distance. "He talked about you, some. He said he noticed we were getting to be good friends. He said he was glad you were getting out of the house these days. He said you were too quiet, you stay alone too much, you live in your head. He said you make up things that never happened." Silence, rain. "I think he figured out I knew where you were sleeping."

Roy is searching, that is clear. There is a question he wants to ask. Nathan becomes very still, his gaze fixed on a point of the tent. Shivering. The moment, the question, fade. Roy draws him closer. After a while, Nathan says, "I don't want to go back."

Rain. The fact of rain. In his mind Nathan can see the swollen creek rushing by in darkness. He and Roy lie still. Nathan unbuttons Roy's shirt to find his body. Roy breathes from deep inside. At first he simply allows the touch, holding Nathan as if he is fragile. But Nathan touches insistently, and the need in him wells up through his hands.

It is awkward, even funny, to undress him and make love to him in the tent. Roy's body has become a customary object, even the tastes are familiar. In the tent, in the dark, Nathan makes him laugh and cry out loud, a power of nighttime, and the look on Roy's face at the end is like food, Nathan hovers over him.

The rain washes, the white sound cleanses, the woodland expands.

Later Roy asks, "Do you mind when I don't do the same thing back to you?"

"No, I don't mind." But at that moment he begins to wonder if he does.

The earth makes a softer bed than Nathan expected. They lie against each other, loosely threaded together, and soon Roy's breath changes, deepens. Nathan lies awake a little longer, his body's rhythm gradually slowing to match Roy's. A dark heaviness overtakes him at last, and his thinking washes away in the sound of rain. In his dreams he and Roy are buying horses, beautiful dark-coated animals, and riding across gardens of goldenrod, yarrow, chicory, and ironweed, with a view of mountains blue-veiled in the distance.

Chapter Ten

When he wakens, a soft darkness fills the interior of the tent, different from the hard shadow of night. Somewhere there is an eastern sky and it has begun to lighten. Roy's face is nested in Nathan's hair, the slackness of his mouth wetting Nathan's throat. The smell of his breath, of his skin, pervades Nathan; odd, how sweet it is, to smell this boy from so close. They are bound together by the weight of Roy's leg across Nathan's thighs, by Roy's arm across Nathan's chest. They are, they have been, all night, one flesh. Joining them further is the heaviness of Roy's erection in his white shorts, which he presses against Nathan's thigh. Its presence has become almost another kind of protection.

Roy murmurs and stirs. The long leg stretches, flexes, pulls Nathan closer. The one sleeping bag in which they have wrapped themselves falls away. Nathan admires the detail of the boy that he can now see, the fine, dark hair along the legs, the line of arms and shoulders. For a moment another image intrudes into his peace, a memory of older, whiter, fallen flesh, of grizzled hair and oily skin, of a sour smell and the feeling of suffocation. But the edge of memory comes without panic this time, and Nathan, as he has learned to do, focuses on the next breath, the cool of the morning in which his heart is currently beating. The memory dissolves. He closes the door and locks it. Nothing more will escape.

Outside, Randy sings a country music love song while banging the frying pan on a rock.

After a few moments, Roy groans and stretches. He kisses Nathan sweetly, murmurs a good morning. Randy's song continues, and Roy sings with him, in a clear voice, lighter than Nathan would have expected.

Again from outside comes Burke's booming baritone calling all lazy good-for-nothings to climb out of their sleeping bags.

Dressing is a clumsy process in the tent, but Nathan is too shy to carry his clothes outdoors as Roy does. Nathan buttons his shirt, zips his pants. Outside the woodland shimmers with clear light and shaggy, vaulted green, branches hung with jagged banners of sweet autumn clematis. The air smells of bee balm, vaguely like mint and medicine, and carries the freshness of the morning after a storm. Even the creek now moves less brackishly, and some daylight penetrates a lining of moss and mud. Nathan walks along the creek bank, kneels and touches the chilly water.

Burke and Randy have made breakfast already, the bacon less burned than for supper. Roy has brought instant coffee, and Nathan drinks it from Roy's tin cup, which becomes almost too hot to touch. The closeness in which they have rested through the night continues to surround them during the breakfast, a peace that fills the space between them, almost visible. There is a softness in Roy's eyes when he watches Nathan, and for Nathan the feeling is perfected in some way; Roy anchors him in the present, strips away shadows of the past. Like breathing, in and out. Nathan basks in the beating of his own heart, in the descending calls of birds, in the fresh shadows of leaves on the backs of his hands. Life becomes a cool gentleness, a process of listening, a caressing presence. In the world that exists only through Roy.

Maybe the feeling is so palpable that even Randy and Burke are aware of it. Especially Burke. He sits across from Nathan at the campfire and watches with lowered eyes.

They strike camp quickly. Roy dismantles and packs the tent, and the memories of the night before are stowed away as quickly. Nathan helps Randy with the cooking equipment while Burke splashes water on the fire and buries the ashes.

Roy stands with his pack set over his shoulders, waiting.

Breezes lift the lower branches in the glade, stir the yellowing fronds of ferns, the wisteria, the bluehearts, moss, and tangles of honeysuckle, and sun strikes everything, and scents rise like waves of heat.

Without a word, Roy ascertains that all is ready and sets out walking. Taking a deep breath, Nathan follows.

Their path follows the creek through several turns to a place where a long, narrow island almost bisects it. Stones form a natural ford to the island. Roy warns Nathan to be careful on the slick backs; he himself steps nimbly to the mossy shore and picks a path to the other side. He moves with certainty, as if the landmarks here are well known to him. Nathan admires his graceful lancing through the underbrush. Nathan pauses in a stand of tall green ferns. Roy has already crossed to the opposite shore and waits in the grass beyond. "You can jump," Roy calls, "it's pretty narrow."

Nathan takes a running start at a slant and flies over the dark water. Roy catches him by the elbow. There is intimacy in the moment, in the way Roy touches Nathan. "Now we go this way," Roy says, and when Nathan turns, there is Burke, watching.

They leave the course of the creek, and tall pines open the roof of the forest to light and sky. Walking becomes easy, one has only to be mindful of cones and dry branches. The cool morning lends quickness to their steps. In the airy vaults Randy sings again, a hymn from the *Broadman Hymnal*, *Up from the grave he arose, with a mighty triumph o'er his foes*, and there is something clear in his voice, not echoing but rather expanding and dissolving into the trees. Roy, ahead, moves without weight. Burke, sometimes behind Nathan and sometimes beside him, scowls at the earth, tramping on pine cones and fallen leaves.

They move through a darker, denser part of the

woods, where oak and maple claim territory from the pines and where the underbrush becomes more compact, a mass of vine, leaf, and wild blossom. The ground rises in rolling slopes, and the footing is sometimes treacherous, over dewy growth or thick moss. The forest is all-engulfing, a vast canopy and airy castle of trees, splendid, unimaginable. Nathan's heart pounds. The dim-lit terrain rolls by, more alien with each step. Dead trees twist toward the sky, hung with garlands of sweet autumn clematis studded with seed heads gossamer as spider's egg sacs. The stillness affects all the boys, and Randy stops his singing. Roy continues to lead, his back sliding deftly through corridors of branches. Burke, meanwhile, walks closer to Nathan than before, and sometimes Nathan can almost feel his breath on his neck.

The path Roy promised soon appears. In fact it is not a path at all but the remnants of Poke's Road, an extension long forgotten, that once bisected the Kennicutt Woods. Honeysuckle has filled the ditch on one side and the other is overgrown with cattail and fern. Its course can be followed, although the roadbed has been retaken by the growth of grass and wild roses, thorn-studded and heavy. They pick their way carefully forward, swinging the branches aside with arcs of their arms. Above, the glimmering sky lightens beyond the laces of leaves, shadows shifting like a kaleidoscope.

They walk forward. Nathan's heart is pounding, and something like awe is rising in him, at the fact of the road and its destination but also at the eerie familiarity. Something prickles in the image, as if he already knows the place. The fall of light along a patch of broken fence strikes him as something he has seen before, there at the place where Roy is standing.

Further on, like a golden curtain, poplars stand in an airy thicket. Sunlight pours straight through the tender trunks.

Soon the road parallels another running stream. The boys follow them both till late morning, when Roy halts the march. The heat has begun to thicken under the broad shade.

"We ought to rest for a while," Roy says, stripping off his backpack and sprawling on the ground, "there's a ways further to go."

Randy lounges beside Roy while Burke ranges along the creek bank, where a bed of fern brushes his jeans. He runs his hands through his hair and scratches his chest. He paces up and down the clearing. When he turns, he is behind Roy and Randy, watching Nathan.

"It's hot as hell," Burke says.

"Sure is."

Randy hums, *There is a place of quiet rest, near to the heart of God.*

Burke scratches his chest under the shirt, then unbuttons the shirt and takes it off. His eyes are blank and flat, as if made of glass. But he still watches Nathan. He stands behind Roy and Randy, who do not see him.

His body is strong. He is bigger than he looks in the shirt. He has dense, square, ungraceful muscles, and a dark patch of hair in the cleft of his chest. His arms are thick and brawny, and he stretches them upward in the sunlight. His expression never changes. Nathan, embarrassed, looks away, then quickly back again. Burke is still watching, stretching his arms, shaking them, then finally turning away himself, kneeling at the side of the creek and splashing his face with water.

Nathan's heart suddenly pounds, and he takes a seat near Roy, though not as near Roy as he might have.

Burke stands with the sun falling over his bare shoulders.

Randy says, "This place is a little spooky."

"People don't come down here too much." Roy chews a blade of grass. "My Uncle Heben brought me out here, when I was little."

"Where?" Burke asked, idly twisting his forearms.

"There's an old farm at the end. With a big house. Nobody lives there anymore."

Something about the simple description causes them all to peer down the road. The promise of an abandoned house. "How far?" Nathan asks.

Their eyes do meet. The softness of Roy surrounds Nathan. "We still got a good ways to walk."

Burke bends over the pack he has been carrying on his shoulders, and when he straightens he is holding the clear flat bottle, half-full of whiskey. He curls the bottle to his mouth.

The prickle in Nathan's scalp makes him stand, suddenly, walking to another part of the clearing. Roy watches, puzzled.

Burke says, "I like a drink of liquor. You want one, Randy?"

"Not yet."

"Roy?"

"Nope."

Burke laughs. "Fine. More for me I guess." And curls his arm again.

Nathan turns to Roy, who is standing. Roy says, "It's time to walk," and slings his pack over his shoulders. Nathan follows him to the remains of the road, as Randy scrambles to his feet.

Burke, eyeing Nathan, screws the top on the bottle, shoving it into his pocket. He clears his throat. He has tied the shirt around his waist. There is something about the display of his body, the arrogance of it, that troubles Nathan.

Burke, ambling forward, drapes an arm around Randy's shoulder. His bulk engulfs even Randy's pale plumpness. "You should have a drink, old buddy."

"Later."

Burke winks at Roy. "I'm ready, Cap'm Roy."

Roy frowns.

"Wish I was in the land of cotton," Burke sings.

Then they are all walking again, forward through the high grass along the bed of the old road, with the creek beside them and the wind in the old trees. The walk stretches through the rest of the morning and into early afternoon. At times Poke's Road nearly disappears, so overgrown has it become. They walk forward in a hot October, with Roy leading in his white tee shirt, and Burke close by him, displaying his broad bare shoulders, like a challenge.

They reach a sharp curve and then, beyond, a twin row of oak trees flanking a broad lane. Sections of fence have tumbled along the ditch. At one point, the remains of a footbridge have partly collapsed into the running water of the creek. Some of the sentinel oaks are dying; Roy points them out. Last night's storm has tossed one grandfather to its side across the road. A raw gash rips the earth beneath the upraised roots. Man-thick branches are splintered in the air, oozing orange. The ground has a startled look.

"Must have been some wind," Randy says.

"It was some wind all right," Roy answers.

Burke stares into the plate of earth and roots, the shadow of which falls across his slightly dull expression. He scratches his hairy navel with a finger, then ambles ahead swinging his arms. Roy waits for Nathan to step away from the fallen tree.

Burke, near the road, feints an attack on Randy, then grabs him from behind, gets him in a headlock and grinds his arm on Randy's head, Burke gritting his teeth, sunlight cascading over his brown shoulders. He pulls Randy this way and that by the head. Randy, enraged, shoves Burke violently away and Burke staggers forward, laughing mildly.

Randy says, "You always try to hurt somebody."

Burke laughs into his fist.

Handing Burke his pack, Roy steps between them. Randy is still breathing heavily, glaring at Burke. Roy says, "You all right?"

"Shit, yes, he's all right, I ain't done nothing to him." Burke rips the pack from Roy's hand and straps it over his shoulders. Adjusting the weight, settling it over his arms.

"I'm fine," Randy says. "He just likes to be too rough all the time."

Burke has stepped ahead again. Roy, for the first time, follows.

Ahead, as if posed, Burke in a pool of sunlight studies the two halves of an iron gate, a stone wall.

Chapter Eleven

Beyond the gate is a lane, now thick with weeds and undergrowth; Nathan recognizes a stand of blackberry bushes and a tangle of wild roses, out of bloom. At the end of the tangled lane, glimpsed beneath lowering branches, hangs a shadow, a broad sagging porch and slatted window shutters.

Roy flanks the vision now, and looks Nathan in the eye. "This is what I wanted to show you. I never brought anybody here before."

"This is a plantation house," Burke says. "My dad told me about this place. He saw it one time when he was hunting."

Roy chews the end of broomstraw.

Randy says, "I didn't know there was ever any plantation out here."

"Some of the Kennicutts owned it," Roy says. "Their graves are out yonder in the trees. They cleared out the woods around here a way long time ago. They were kin to the people who had the place where our farm is, but that place burned down and the land got sold."

"And they all just left this place." Randy is gazing upward, at the vague outline of a roof beyond high treetops.

"It never did pass for much. That's what my dad said."

The first sight of the ruin, when they pass the oaks that obscure the mansion's breadth, take Nathan aback. He has never seen a house as large as this, and it rivals, for bulk, the federal courthouse in Gibsonville and the elementary school in Potter's Lake. Wooden columns support wide plank porches that surround both floors of the house. The wood has weathered uniformly gray, windows shuttered or broken, doors mutely closed. Dormer windows peer out from the attic. A tree has fallen across one of the side porches, shards of roof timber littering the overgrown yard beneath. The signs of damage are old; this did not happen last night.

They pick a path along the side of the house, beneath the shuttered windows and sagging porches. The stillness of the house lends an eerie sense of waiting to the walk, not as if the house is truly empty but as if its inhabitants are all hiding, or watching. Nathan remembers Roy mentioning a haunted house in the Kennicutt Woods and realizes, with a sense of wonder, that this must be the place.

They cross what had been the front lawn, leading down to a place where the creek widens over smooth rocks. By now the afternoon is waning.

"We should spend the night here," Roy says.

"In the house?" Randy gazes at the huge bulk, perplexed.

"No. We can camp down by the creek."

"Good. I know I don't want to sleep in that house."

Nathan is also disturbed by the prospect. The tent and open air seem more inviting.

"This place is supposed to be haunted," Roy says, sounding wary. "My Uncle Heben says it was in a book about North Carolina ghosts. There was a picture of this house. The last full-blood Kennicutt who lived here got killed by one of his slaves, and they cut his head off. So he still walks around the place at night looking for his head."

"You're full of shit," Randy says.

They look around at the somber setting. They stand in the remains of the front yard now, thick with poplars and privet; they are facing the house, within the broad curve of the carriageway, behind wildly overgrown hedges that border the approach to the main doors. The facade of the house has graceful lines, and there is something hospitable, inviting, about the spacious porches and broad doors, even given the present state of decay. It seems less like a mansion than some pleasant farmhouse that grew larger than expected. If it is haunted, the afternoon sun reveals nothing of its ghosts. But even so, the boys accept the facts as Roy presents them, that he has an Uncle Heben who once saw a picture of this house. That a headless ghost is said to roam the grounds, in a story famous enough to have been published in a book. They will sleep tonight in sight of a haunted place.

Burke gazes at the house with an expression of serenity, a peaceful emptiness.

They set up camp within sight of the main doors, near the creek, and sunset strikes a kind of bronze glow from the decay. As if the grass were burning. Amid the late-afternoon changes of light and shadow, they set up tents. Roy finds rocks for the fire circle. Nathan heads off to gather wood and Randy follows. The two work quietly in the diminishing light, mindful of their noise as if they are in church, or in the library at school. Because of Randy's size, he has a hard time with the wood, the sticks and branches digging into the softness of his belly. He works without complaint, sweating as if it is summer, humming softly, *Just as I am without one plea*. Nathan finds himself humming too. The soft sound connects the two boys. Randy's air of gentleness makes Nathan feel welcome in his presence, though they hardly speak. They return to the campsite with armloads of kindling and branches, the driest wood they can find.

Burke splits the wood with a short ax, and the late sun falls over him from the west, flashes of warmth along his shoulders and back. He stacks the split wood, and Randy helps, till soon they have plenty for the night's fire. Most of it is dry enough to burn, Burke says, and wipes the sweat from his forehead. He winks at Nathan over Roy's head.

They eat supper early, with the sun setting at their

backs. After cleanup, deep into dusk, they go exploring in the grounds behind the big house. In the overgrown yard beyond what was once a kitchen garden, they find a stone barn, doors hanging off the hinges, flaked with what remains of a deep blue paint. Inside the shell of the house, grass has overtaken the dirt floor, and the lofts have collapsed along the walls. Bats and swallows live in the rafters, darting in and out of a gaping hole in the roof. Behind the barn is a dairy and another long, low building near the wreck of a paddock fence. They recognize this as a stable by the layout of horse stalls and the remains of a wagon wheel, spokes rotted inside the iron rim. Nathan finds a bit of leather harness in the grass near one of the stalls, the soft leather coming to pieces in his hand.

Beyond the stable, down a just discernible path, stands a row of shacks. Most are still intact, though the roofs have rotted away, but one or two have collapsed to heaps of gray clapboard. Eerie, the street of some deserted town. Roy says these were the slave houses, a notion that sobers Nathan.

Out past the shacks lie the once cleared fields of the farm, long since overgrown. One day even the house, even the stone barn, will be reclaimed by the forest. Amber light floods the grounds, almost horizontal, like a tide. Among the long shadows of trees and the burning of color against sun bleached wooden walls they wander. The silence of the place draws them close together, and by sunset they are walking almost shoulder to shoulder in the purpled light. They halt at the edge of a grove of cedars, outside of a low iron fence that bounds a patch of high grass. "My Uncle Heben said this was where they buried the slaves, right here. They buried the family somewhere else." Nathan finds the gate and steps through it. The grass is waist high, and he picks his way forward carefully. He is well within the fence before he realizes he has come exploring alone; the others are gaping at him from the last of twilight. He stands in the murk under the trees.

Nathan has spent so much time, lately, among the dead Kennicutts, he feels almost at home here among their chattel. But he finds not even a single gravestone to read; he finds no sign of graves here at all. He stares down at the grass as if waiting for a hand to reach upward, or for a voice to call out from the ground. He wonders how they marked the graves, if they did. Maybe with wooden crosses, as in Western movies. Maybe the evidence is here, unseen, beneath the grass. He waits. The others are watching, holding their breath.

Retreating carefully, he joins them. He is acutely aware of his feet. He has a feeling the graves are crowded together and one must be careful. Though he is aware of no fear, he is relieved when he clears the fence and stands with the others again. They are gaping at him as if he has done something extraordinary. "There's nothing in there, you can't tell where the graves are."

"They were slaves," Roy says.

"But there's a fence. Why would they put up a fence if they wouldn't even mark the graves?"

"This is creepy." Randy looks around the dark grove

of trees as if waiting for one of the shadows to begin to move.

"It's getting pretty dark." Burke reaches for his flask again. It is almost too dark to watch him drink.

"A ghost will haunt you in the day time just like it will at night," Randy says, "that's what my Aunt Ida told me one time. She says it's a superstition that a ghost will only get you at night. A ghost will get you in the daytime just as quick. If it's a real ghost." He pauses. "But I still don't want to stand around here."

They study their whereabouts carefully, for any signs of suspicious movement. But the graves are still, and the air is still, and the leaves on the branches of the trees are still. The evening weighs down on them. They move reverently away, and no one says anything at all until they reach the stone barn.

"I bet this place is haunted too," Burke says. No one asks why he thinks so. He sips from the narrow bottle again, this time offering to no one.

Dusk passes to twilight. The ruin of the farmyard looks different now. Vast as the shadow of a mountain, the mansion exudes an air of vigilance, as if there are eyes at every window, peering through the shutters. To reach their campsite they will have to dare a walk through inky darkness close to the house, through high grass where they cannot be certain where they are stepping. Amid the wild cries of cicadas, bats, distant owls, they drift forward uncertainly.

"I wish we had a flashlight," Randy says.

"I brought one but I left it in my pack," Roy answers. "You guys ain't scared, are you?"

"No, I just wish I could see what I'm stepping on." But a slight tremor in Randy's voice betrays him.

They fall silent. The night's harsh chorus rises. Nathan steps toward the shadow. It is safe, in the darkness, to pause near Roy, to inhale his familiar smells. They are close, for a moment, in the overgrown yard; they are almost touching, and no one can see.

"Let me know if you get scared, Nathan." Burke's voice is full of scorn.

Nathan steps past Roy, into the shadow of the big house. He refuses to turn. The others can follow, or not. He vanishes into the blackest shadow of his life.

The cool darkness lends his motion a feeling of gliding. He is a fish slipping through water, he remains very calm. Soon he can hear the others following, and he smiles to think he has gone first, even ahead of Roy. Breathtaking, to walk so close the house, to slide through air as if it were water, headed toward vague light that is more and more like mist or cloud. To step past tangled branches, to lift them aside. Who knows how many eyes are there, watching from the black space around him? He listens, and it seems to him the silence of the house engulfs the sound of the others; now he can only hear the ringing emptiness of the house beside him. The emptiness beckons him, as clearly as if it is calling his name. Again comes the sensation that the passage of time has been slowed or stopped. That he will never leave this darkness.

He is hardly aware of walking anymore. The house breathes beside him. His heart is pounding.

When he bursts into the twilight of the yard and can see again, he finds himself surprised, as if he had expected to be blind like that for a much longer time. He is gasping; he has been holding his breath. He moves forward, taking gulps of air. Overhead, stars slash and burn in a fiery sky, early night. The other boys emerge behind him. They are breathless, too, as they rush toward the creek. The bulk of the house waits, silent and cold beneath a crown of stars.

The three close on Nathan, and there is something brotherly in their buffets of affection. "That was great," Randy says. "Jesus."

"I could swear something was touching me," Roy says.

"Me too."

"It was like there was something in the house looking at us. I could feel it."

"We should go in there," Burke says. "We should go in the house."

Silence.

"We should." He sets his jaw and looks at Roy. They cannot meet each other's eyes. Burke is breathing hard.

"What's the matter? You don't think there's a real ghost in there."

"I ain't scared even if there is a ghost." Roy speaks calmly.

"How about you?"

"I'm not scared, I just don't want to go in there," says Randy.

"Chicken shit."

"You damn right I'm chicken shit." But he stares at the house, fascinated. He licks his lip. "You think it would be all right? You think we can get in?"

Burke laughs. He eyes Nathan up and down. "What about you?"

Nathan faces the house, tracing its shadow against the sky. "Going inside is fine with me."

Roy faces Burke belligerently. "See, asshole? Nobody's scared. The only thing I'm thinking about is we'd have to be careful. That house is liable to come down around your head if you step in the wrong place. It's dark and we won't be able to see. It's dangerous."

"Oh yeah? Well, I say you're scared. That's what it looks like to me."

They glare at each other. Roy holds his place, quiet and determined. He is a match for Burke, Nathan thinks. But Burke carries himself more aggressively, his chin juts toward Roy and trembles. His face flushes with emotion.

Nathan still faces the house. "It's a full moon. If we wait a little bit, there'll be plenty of light."

Roy is watching him, Nathan can feel it. But Nathan holds fast to the house, faces that direction, and breathes the scent of late blooming jasmine.

Roy studies the sky. He leans close, a warm presence. "You really want to do this?"

"That's what he said."

"I'm asking him." Waiting then.

"Why does he get to decide?"

But still Roy is silent. The moment is rich. Nathan can taste each fluttering of Roy's pulse, each rise of scent from his body. "It would be fun."

Roy scratches behind one ear. When he begins to smile, the tension eases. "Well, I know I don't want to go in that front door. We'll never get it open."

Burke and Randy laugh. "All right," Burke says, "we won't go in that way."

Randy, generously, adds, "You know the house, Roy. How do we get inside?"

Secure in his leadership, Roy studies the problem. The rising moon brings soft light to the lawn, illuminating the overgrown azaleas along the sweep of what was once a front yard. Eerie white glaze obscures the windows and washes the facade. "There's a door at the side. And there's broken windows. And there's doors at the back, too. Me and Uncle Heben tried a door back there. But we couldn't open it."

"Did you get in?"

"We could of climbed in a window. But Uncle Heben changed his mind."

"He probably got scared, too," Randy says.

"Maybe. It was a long time ago. I don't remember."

They all stare at the house somberly. Burke walks toward it a few steps. This time he passes the flask to the others, and everyone drinks but Nathan. The moment has come. Roy finds his flashlight. "Just in case we need it," he explains. They trot across the yard in the moonlight, Roy leading. They are all following in no order, but Nathan runs close to Roy.

Beyond the layers of trees, white as anything, a full moon blazes. The ivory face threatens to make day, even glimpsed in pieces through branches. Nathan sees a woman in the glittering, the face of a woman staring into a high wind of whiteness, and soon she will be clearing the trees and rising into a sky filled with stars.

They travel in the shadow of the house. The size of the place surprises Nathan again as they approach. How could people need so much room? In the darkness the shuttered windows are like lidded eyes. It is a different feeling, to approach with the knowledge that they are going inside. The darkness seems darker, the sense of invisible presences more acute. They halt a moment at the foot of the stone steps leading to the main porch. Roy checks the windows nearby, slipping fearlessly up the steps and along the porch, sliding his hands along the shutters. Nathan's heart is pounding, but he keeps his eyes on Roy. From shadow to shadow he moves, and the others move parallel to him along the side of the house. He returns further along and whispers, as if they are all concealing themselves from something inside, "Everything's nailed shut. Like I remembered."

They reach the place where the tree has fallen against the house, and once there they climb onto the porch and review the wreckage. Roy clambers over the old tree trunk, peers at the splintered wood of the porch above their heads, the one that circles the second floor of the house. The bulk of the tree rests there. "The tree's leaning on the house," Roy whispers, "It didn't bust through."

"The windows?" Burke asks. "I bet it knocked some loose."

"Looks like it could have."

"You want to try up there?"

Roy considers. His face lost in the shadows of the tree. "Not yet. We can come back if we don't find something better."

Beyond the tree, they enter a fenced garden that runs the length of the house, adjoining the place where the house swells out and the porches stop.

Through the shadows of the trees they can see the stone barn and some of the outbuildings. The trees thin near that part of the house and the moonlight falls through in showers of whiteness, clear and clean. The whole farmyard is etched, as if a portrait of itself, a study of wreckage of what was once inhabited. They pick their way through the garden, where the night carries a thousand smells. Nathan is mindful of snakes underfoot, though not quite sure what to do if he steps on one. Roy keeps them to a path that he seems to know, at the same time scanning the house carefully.

"We can't get to these windows, they're too high," he says. "Too bad. Half of them are broke."

"This is weird," Randy says. "Look at this place. What kind of garden was this?"

"You still want to go inside?"

146

"Oh yeah." But he studies the shadowy garden nevertheless.

"Do you?" Burke asks Roy.

"You bet." By now they are crossing the back of the house, in full moonlight, through waist-high grass.

The stark outline of the house leaves Nathan breathless. The upper floor swims out of darkness into stark clarity, so well illuminated he can count the cracks in the outer boards. A porch encircles the kitchen building and then crosses by means of a short gallery to the main house. Roy tests the porch, finds it will hold them. They follow him.

Now they are close to the house, sliding along the walls, near the shuttered windows. Roy still leads, though now Burke has claimed the place beside him. Randy and Nathan follow. It occurs to Nathan that with the windows shuttered the fact of moonlight will make no difference inside, the house will be very dark. But he says nothing. They cross the gallery to what must have been a door for kitchen servants.

"This is the door me and Uncle Heben tried." Roy's tone is quite soft, though not a whisper. "Now it's boarded up."

They follow along the porch, their footsteps ringing. They walk more quietly, each without prompting. They find stairs and Roy tests them. One is broken but the next is sound. They climb to the second-story porch now, and with each step they sink into the quiet shroud of the house.

The porch is solid in most places, and they move

with confidence. They cross the front of the house again, then along the side gallery, where the windows are also shuttered. At places the porch protests their weight and they space themselves by the sounding of the floorboards. The floor holds despite its protests. Roy has brought a flashlight but uses it sparingly.

They pause to study the darkness in the direction of their camp. Not even ghost embers of their campfire can be seen.

On the other side of the house, where the tree has fallen, they find a window with shutters that have been partially loosened. It takes both Burke and Roy to pry the shutter open. Roy makes the first attempt, alone, and then Burke tries, alone. They are watching each other, each hoping the other will not succeed. Nathan is near enough to admire the moonlight along Roy's straining arms, the snake-play of muscle along Burke's back. Their separate efforts fail, and they position themselves to work together. Roy, affecting that he will dirty his tee shirt, takes it off. But instead of looping it through his belt, he hands it to Nathan.

Nathan takes the shirt. Roy stretches his shoulders a little. The moment is small and passes easily beneath the awareness of the others. Burke and Roy pry the shutter free of its remaining nails and swing it slowly on its hinges. The wooden frame is still solid and the shutter soon lies flat against the house as it used to do.

Roy shines the flashlight and carefully brushes away the remains of old glass from the windowsill. His bare back drains a streak of moon down the spine. Burke, near him, drinks from the flask again, offers to Randy, offers to Roy. Roy straightens from the windowsill, takes the bottle and flashes a warm grin to Nathan. He lifts the bottle. He is beautiful to Nathan, he is clearly aware of the fact. The swallow of liquor becomes a performance. He wipes his mouth and hands the bottle to Burke. Then he leaps through the window.

Burke follows him the next moment, with a look of reckless bravery; but he is still only the second one to enter, he has been diminished by Roy. Randy clambers over. Because he is thick-waisted, to get inside takes effort, and he breathes heavily; though maybe this is as much from fear as from exertion. Nathan slides over the windowsill, careful of the glass. His heart is pounding. They are inside the house.

The room they have entered is small and oddly shaped. From inside one can hardly tell the fallen tree is there. The place would be pitch dark except for the flashlight, which Roy washes over the floor. Randy takes a step and the floorboards groan but hold steady. The boys walk carefully.

They go through a door and then down a hallway, and suddenly they are steeped in moonlight. They are standing at the top of the gallery overlooking a grand staircase. From a skylight overhead, partially broken, wind rattles through empty panes. Moonlight falls strong from there, and the vaulted space floods with light. The lower floor is dark.

Beyond the sound of the wind, is there something else? A thread of music suggests itself to Nathan, who follows the melody in his head. As if someone with a clear voice is singing softly in a distant room. He misses the words, but the sound is very pure.

Roy keeps the flashlight at his side, in spite of the darkness. They pick their way forward carefully. The floor is solid all the way to the top of the stairs, and the stairs seem solid too, but there is the hole in the skylight and a pool of water beneath it. One can see the water from the gallery, a patch of reflection in the deep darkness. The four of them stand at the top of the stairs looking at each other.

"We should explore up here first." Randy's tone makes it clear that he is reluctant to descend into that well of darkness.

"But after that, we have to go down there." Burke squares his shoulders.

The rooms on the second floor are small and plain, like the rooms in any farmhouse Nathan has ever seen. The floors have held up, though the boards sag in a few places and groan in many. The rooms have a desolate feeling, containing little beyond scraps of furniture, the chimney from an old gas lantern, a tin plate with a bit of candle. In one room, beside an unshuttered window, they find a nearly whole chair, casting its long moon shadow across dust and cobwebs. It has a delicate look, like something that might once have faced a woman's vanity table, with slender, curved legs and one thin, spidery arm. Beneath the cake of dust that shields the cushion is a dark stain. Roy uses the flashlight here for the first time, and they see the startling pink of the cushion, the patina of dust. The dark stain's resemblance to old blood is unnerving; even Burke, buffeted by his bravura, seems wary at the sight. "I wonder why they left this," he says. "They took everything else."

"That's blood, ain't it?" Randy asks.

"It looks like it might be." Roy's answer is bland.

"Maybe this is the room where the slave cut the master's head off," Nathan suggests, and they all look at him.

"Jesus."

"Or maybe not." Nathan looks around. "There would be a lot more blood than just this."

That is enough for the others. They head out of the room, all but Nathan. He goes on standing there. He finds a place in the wallpaper, another stain like a bloody hand outlined in a pane of moonlight thrown from the window. "There's another stain," he says. "Maybe this is the right room, after all."

Nor is he teasing them, entirely. He is seeing the room a different way. His hands glide along the back of the chair, and when he realizes where he is again, he is counting strands of spider web on the fireplace mantel.

Then without another thought he carries the chair to the fireplace and sets it at an angle to one side. He lifts it by the remaining arm. He studies the chair from behind, as if judging its placement. Then he backs away.

They stay perfectly still and take deep breaths.

"Why did you do that?" Roy asks.

Nathan blinks. The question strikes him as odd. "I think it looks better there."

"He's fucking with us." Burke stands with his fists clenched.

"I'm not fucking with anybody."

Roy laughs and then Randy follows his lead. His body tense, Burke glares at Nathan.

"Let's go." Roy leads them out of the room.

The rest of the rooms they visit are bare, and they find no other evidence of occupation, neither ghostly nor otherwise; except, near the door of one room, Nathan discovers a doll's foot made of thick porcelain and covered with dust. He cleans it, white and pink, on the tail of his shirt. Nathan turns the foot around and around in his hand. Then, without asking anybody, he replaces the porcelain foot in the dust, in the same position as before, but clean and shining.

They find narrow stairways leading to the attic, these at the back of the house, open to access; and they find service stairways leading down, also at the back of the house; but the entrances are boarded off beyond a couple of steps. They enter many rooms full of dirt and dust, spider webs and leaves, branches and dead birds, bits of broken glass.

Nathan still hears the music, the tiny sound like singing at the back of all the other sounds, the creaking floors and the house settling, the wind through broken windows. He can tell the others are listening like he is and he wonders, he is suspicious that they are hearing other songs. Maybe they are even getting the words too.

When they have explored the upper level, they return to the grand central corridor, the skylight and descending stairs. They have turned off the flashlight again and are walking in the ambient light; the moon has risen higher, and the whole space is bathed in milk.

Below they can see the outlines of a large entry hall at the end of the long curved stair. Vague outlines of door-ways and rooms beyond are visible, as if they are being invited. They descend without discussion. Nathan follows Roy, claiming that place for himself. He knots Roy's tee shirt in his hand, as if for luck or protection. They step carefully down the speaking stairs where the darkness absorbs them gradually. Soon Nathan can see the outlines of the room, larger than any he has ever entered, larger even than the sanctuary at church or the auditorium at school. A layer of dirt and leaves carpets the floor, which slants toward the pool of water. Water drips into the pool from above, a periodic sound that echoes. "That floor is about gone," Roy says.

But to the left rises a tall, broad archway, the pale beams of the arch outlined in moonlight. The room beyond is dark, but engulfs sound like a large space. It is the sound of their footfalls, their breathing and coughing, that it swallows, along with the dripping water. These sounds multiply as if a voice is coursing through Nathan's head, a tiny singing, sometimes clear and sometimes too soft to distinguish. They walk into the room.

Nathan's immediate impression is that he knows the place, even though the shutters are closed, even though the moonlight flickers feebly. The outlines of the room are clear to him. The ceilings are high, a room of generous proportions. Four windows open on one wall and three on another. A fireplace at one end has lost a good deal of tile and brick, bits of which litter the floor beneath, along with animal turds and dry leaves. There are branches, bits of china, fabric of an indeterminate type, piled in one corner. Rags of draperies hang from a window, singed as if burned; but there are no other signs of fire. The remains of wallpaper peel away from the walls, and the wainscoting warps in a place where the windowpane is missing; even the shutters cannot keep out a heavy rain. Some of this he sees in splashes of the flashlight, but the rest is simply there. In what he knows, without asking why.

Beyond this room is another, not as large, and lined with bookshelves. The shelves are bare save for a city of spiders that has settled on the shelving. Ivy has burst through a window and creeps along the walls.

"What's that smell?" Randy asks Roy.

"Sulfur."

"How do you know?" Burke demands.

"I know what sulfur smells like."

"The Devil is supposed to smell like sulfur," Nathan says.

"Oh that's really funny." Randy sounds more nervous than ever.

Scowling, Burke tips his bottle one last time, almost hidden in the darkness; and this time when he finishes, none is left.

"Where do we go now?"

"Randy, do you have to talk so much?"

"I ain't talking to you, I'm talking to Roy. I just want to know."

But in some way they all share Burke's feeling, that no one should speak. Light from the broken window where ivy grows laces the floor. The ivy leaves are dark like blood on the walls, a deeper shadow. The boys stand there. The room echoes.

They move forward uneasily. Through another archway they step into a room so dark they cannot see the vaguest outline. Either there are no windows or the shutters are airtight. The air is motionless. Roy picks a path carefully, and Nathan follows. Burke is behind him, breathing onto the back of his neck. Randy is last and noisiest, breathing heavily.

They are all increasingly aware of a want for quiet. As if something in the room, or in the rooms beyond, is listening.

A prickle up Nathan's spine. The distant singing has ceased.

It is hard to say which is more complete, the silence or the darkness. They remain motionless somewhere in space, in a room no contour of which is visible.

"Why don't you use the flashlight?" Randy asks.

"Because I don't want to," Roy whispers, "keep quiet."

Somewhere in the heart of the house. They are close enough to one another that they share warmth and the feeling of safety in numbers. The intuition that someone is listening becomes palpable, and Nathan finally senses a direction, a particular place in the darkness. Nathan touches Roy's arm and points.

They can barely see each other. But Roy reads the touch as a message and they head where Nathan points.

They sense the approach of the wall and then, arms out, Roy touches the jamb of a wide doorway.

Nathan can feel the door frame, the space beyond, as black as the one they are leaving.

Randy lets out a deep breath, as good as a plea for the flashlight, but he dares not ask.

The sound of their breathing fills the room, and Nathan wonders whether the sound of other breath might underlie their own. Someone could be standing in the center of that spacious darkness, someone attentive and silent like them. Listening.

Roy edges forward. The others follow.

The air is stale. Burke follows close behind Nathan. His body radiates heat.

Roy freezes.

There is a figure ahead. They can see the outline of a shadow, a broad-shouldered man standing perfectly still. Nathan cannot determine whether or not he has his head.

The figure is visible even in the darkness of the room, and they are very close to it. Then it slowly raises its arms.

Someone grips Nathan's shoulder, hard.

Roy presses back against Nathan, raising the flashlight.

The figure turns and flees. A silent gliding motion carries it toward further darkness.

The boys remain where they are, hardly breathing.

"Shit," Randy whispers. The single word echoes. They hold their breath. They stand perfectly still, listening.

"Did you see that?" Roy asks Nathan.

Nathan whispers, "Yes," since no one can see him nod his head.

"What was it?"

"I don't know."

"That thing didn't make any noise when it moved," Randy says.

"Shut up," Burke says.

"The fuck I will. It's still out there."

"Shut up." Roy switches on the flashlight without warning. Splashing the yellowish circle methodically, he reveals that they are in a large room with the windows boarded from the inside. The room is as tall as two floors of the house, and the beams of the ceiling cast looping shadows. Leaves and dirt litter the floor. Bare of furnishings, pitch dark, the room shrinks the flashlight beam. Nothing else. No figure of a man, nothing.

At last Roy finds the door again and trains the flashlight on it.

Once they reach it, he cleans cobwebs from the frame with a stick. Spiders are moving along the strands of web. Roy turns off the flashlight, and they wait for a moment while their eyes adjust to the dark.

Again, the sense of someone listening is immediate. Nathan can almost find the direction in the darkness, the place where the shadowed figure has returned out there in the black expanse they have crossed. He searches, but his eyes are still learning to read shadow, he sees nothing in the murk.

"He's there." Nathan's voice hardly carries at all.

"Where? Do you see him?" Roy searches the darkness too.

No, he sees only shadow within shadow. But the one who is listening is there. As if he knows who they are. As if he has known they were coming, as if he was waiting for a sign. No one moves. The silence has filled everything, every space in them.

"Nathan's full of shit," Burke whispers, "there's nothing out there."

"Be quiet."

"I mean it," shoving Nathan forward a little, into the dark space again, "he's trying to scare us. The little sonofabitch. Use the flashlight."

"No. We already used it." Roy barely controls anger in his voice.

"Give it to me then, if you're a coward."

Roy and Burke are suddenly squared against each other in the darkness, blowing, and they lock together.

They are fighting over the flashlight quicker than they could have chosen, it is as if the moment has been waiting for them to find it. They strain back and forth, shoving each other in concentrated silence, convulsive, sudden motions, testing each other's strength. Burke strains to take the flashlight but Roy fiercely grips it. They are grunting, swearing, but the sounds are plush and quiet.

Then, suddenly, a resounding thump from the darkness beyond, followed by the sound of footsteps running toward them. A thrill races up Nathan's spine. Burke tears the flashlight free of Roy's hand. Randy makes a noise and runs, and Burke releases Roy and runs, and then they are all running. Into the darkness.

Nathan is hardly aware that Roy has taken his arm, that Roy is guiding him.

They pass through a doorway, then down a passageway through which moonlight falls in slatted patterns onto dusty floorboards. They are alone now, Roy and he, they have lost the others. Roy stops and pulls Nathan to a halt as well. Breathless, they face each other. He can make out Roy's grin in the shadow that is his face. Roy is listening.

For a moment they hear distant voices, maybe Burke and Randy. Afterward, silence falls again.

"That sure scared the shit out of me," Roy whispers, panting. "Did you really see something?"

Nathan shrugs. Roy rests a hand on Nathan's shoulder, laughing quietly. He is still listening, too.

"My uncle told me he saw a ghost here one time. The one in the book. I didn't believe him."

"You think that's what he saw?"

Roy shrugs. "Who knows? But if it's a ghost, I bet it's that old man. If somebody cut my head off, I would want it back."

"I think it's more ghosts than that."

"How do you know?"

"I don't. But it feels like it. It feels like there's all kind of ghosts."

This makes Roy think again. "Are you trying to scare me now?"

"No." Nathan steps away from him. They are in a black room again, and no moonlight seeps through any shuttered windows here. The room feels small. They withdraw from the doorway to a farther wall, where they know each other by touch, by voice. "But this place does feel like there's people in it. Don't you think so?"

Roy is frowning. "I don't know."

"Did you ever come to a place and feel like you'd been there before?"

The frown deepens. "No." Silence. "Did you? Do you feel like you been here before?"

"Not quite." Whispered so quietly Nathan can hardly hear the words himself. "It's more like I'll never leave."

Then a sound, a footfall. Nearby.

Roy, by his stillness, makes clear that he hears too. "What is it?"

"I thought I heard somebody."

"It's probably the guys."

Then comes the sound again. A step, another. Another.

Too heavy for Randy or Burke. The sound approaches from the corridor beyond.

He draws Roy into the deepest part of shadow. The doorway is a lighter outline of gray against the strangling black of the wall.

Silence. Nathan holds his breath.

A figure in the door. A vaguer shadow. Someone stands there with his legs spread apart. He is sturdy, square-shouldered, like Nathan's Dad when he was younger, like Preacher John Roberts. Like Roy. He is familiar. He makes no sound. He is another blankness of the house, a ghost who could be anyone, living or dead.

The moment broadens in some way, and divides. The sensation is explicit. There are two of Nathan, moving in different directions, and time is no longer a line but a knot, a maze, through which he must pick his way. The figure both remains in the doorway and walks away from it, and Nathan follows in each direction. The figure moves away, and Nathan follows, into the dark corridor, up the stairs, through walls, through ceilings and roofs, upward into air, into heaven and night sky.

But the figure also remains in the doorway and in the haze moves vaguely, like something out of a dream, so that it might be Dad taking off his clothes there or it might be the preacher opening the Bible behind the pulpit on Sunday morning.

And Dad's hand on Nathan's thigh.

The unsteady voice in Nathan's ear whispering, *Do you remember what we did when you were a little boy?*

While overhead the voice of the preacher sails like a wind of itself, *Do you remember what the Lord said unto Abraham?*

In the voice of an angel

The Lord said unto Abraham, Lay not thine hand upon the boy, neither do thou anything unto him: for now I know that thou fearest God.

Then Roy lays his hand on Nathan's shoulder and says, "What do you see? What's wrong?"

The shadow lingers in the vague doorway. The divided moment vanishes, converges.

"I thought I saw somebody."

He can feel Roy searching, can feel his strain. They are fixed together, invisibly linked. Roy's breath repeats itself along Nathan's shoulders and neck. He pulls Nathan to him with sudden fervor, his arms encircling, and there is insistence in his body, taut like a wire, like when he first touched Nathan in the graveyard. For Nathan the feeling is like a wind, scouring, and Nathan finds himself echoing with the gust. Roy jerks him close, almost brutish, and the thing in the doorway watches, and now the thing resembles Dad even more, from when Dad was young and strong; and the feeling is like there is something tearing in Nathan. That Roy can hold him roughly, like this. That he can squeeze too tight. The presence of the thing in the doorway robs the moment of any tenderness. Roy turns Nathan around to face him, Nathan's back is to the door, but he can still feel the thing watching. Roy says, "Don't look. I don't know what it is. But don't look out there anymore."

The plaintive note to the voice reaches Nathan.

They are together in the room. They are standing together, and Roy's hands are insisting, his body is insisting. His mouth crawls along Nathan's face and Nathan is tempted, for the first time, to push him away. There are eyes watching from all sides. Roy's heart pounds beneath Nathan's hand. Nathan sighs, and yields.

The need leaves Roy's body a little at a time, and it is almost as if Nathan erases the tension with his hands, squeezing it out through Roy's shoulders. They are together, they run together a little, their edges softening and blending. At first, for Nathan, resistance and anger prevent any pleasure. But this is Roy, not Dad. They are here together, they are safe.

Then, without a sign, Roy kneels in front of Nathan, and Nathan, dumbstruck, searches for his face in the shadows. Roy unfastens Nathan's pants, lets them down.

"What are you doing?"

Roy's hands slide along the backs of Nathan's thighs. The touch burns through all Nathan's nerves, as if his body senses a new intent. Roy slides his hands down Nathan's thighs. Undershorts glide down.

The shock of contact, Roy's soft mouth. It is as if Nathan's nerves are bursting, a wet heat. He has never felt anything like the touch. Roy's face slides in and out of shadow. Now Nathan has something to think about, other than the fear that someone is there in the darkness, waiting in the doorway in the darkness. Tension drains away. He lets go.

When the flashlight finds them, Roy is still kneeling

in front of Nathan, and Nathan's pants are tangled at his ankles. The flashlight catches Roy's mouth straining over Nathan's heaving abdomen. But at the touch of light Roy freezes, and Nathan opens his eyes.

"So." The voice is Burke's, deep and full of bitterness. "This is what you guys do."

Silence.

"You see it, Randy?"

"Yeah." Disgust.

"Looks like Roy sucks dick pretty good," Burke says.

Roy shoves Nathan away. "Get the fuck out of here," Roy says to the beam of light.

Nathan freezes. He is fumbling with his own clothes. He can still see Roy's face, full of horror.

"Don't stop now."

"Turn off that goddamn thing." Roy stands. His voice is trembling with rage.

Randy says, "Jesus, Roy, you do that to him?"

Roy makes a whimpering sound. He steps over Nathan toward the door. "Get away." His voice strangled.

The flashlight suddenly vanishes.

Footsteps retreat.

Numb. When Nathan turns, Roy's outline hovers in the doorway. It is Roy, the figure is his, was his. Hesitant, one arm on the doorjamb, Roy searches down the hall in the darkness. For a moment there is a fluctuation that Nathan can feel, the possibility of another division of time, so that Roy could both stay and escape. But the moment remains rigorous. Roy vanishes.

Chapter Twelve

He is alone in the dark for a long time, with a wind howling through him.

The house has fallen silent. The vague doorway remains empty. Nathan sits with his hands on his knees. His shirt hangs open, last touched by Roy. The faintest feather of air along his bare skin is his only true sensation.

He has no thoughts for a long time. He sits and breathes. Sketches of past moments return to him, Roy's hands and mouth, the sudden pressure of their bodies, the miracle of reciprocity, and then the abrupt wash of light, the realization that Burke and Randy had found them. Fragments of that sequence recur. Most vivid is when Roy pushes him away. Nathan has stayed frozen in that position ever since.

But these are memories. He can escape them. What he cannot escape is the sensation of wind inside him. There is a torn place somewhere in his gut and wind is rushing through it. A sound, like someone humming a sad hymn, resonates through the hollow.

After a while he realizes he is really humming, and the hymn is "Near to the Heart of God." Quiet rest. The room echoes with his voice.

A prickle along his neck warns him. He turns slowly.

He cannot see anything. Amazing how dark the room remains. But someone waits behind him again. He can hear the breathing this time.

He stands, slowly. His knees are stiff and sore, he must have been sitting for a long time. He faces the place in the darkness from which he hears breathing. Nothing reveals itself, not even a lighter shadow in the inky room. The door has dissolved in the changing fall of moonlight. But something is there, Nathan can hear it.

"Hello." Nathan's voice is a thin thread in the blackness.

A sound, an involuntary step. Something shifting its weight.

"Hello." Nathan steps backward. He tries to feel the direction of the door. He steps again. His heart is pounding.

The sound is distinct this time. The thing comes toward Nathan. Coughs, or clears its throat.

Nathan turns.

Suddenly he has no sense of direction. The doorway, from which moonlight has faded, has become invisible. He takes a step, and the floorboards boards creak dangerously. He stops.

A hand grips him at the elbow.

He makes a low sound and tries to pull away. The hand tightens.

Nathan cannot even hear breathing. "Who are you?"

The hand simply grips him. The hand is very strong, the fingers dig deep into Nathan's arm. For a stunned moment they are motionless. Then Nathan lunges away from the grip at the same moment that the other hand smashes into his face. Across the bridge of the nose. Nathan sags and the hand closes over his eyes. Nathan is being dragged by the shoulders, he is too dazed to move. He hears cloth being ripped, and he realizes he is staring down at something, that his eyes are seeing something, but then a rag wraps around his head.

Blackness within blackness. The cloth binds tight across his eyes. Now he need not even try to see.

He can still hear breathing, ragged now. After the blindfold they are still again, and Nathan waits. The first wave of panic has passed and his thoughts are becoming clear.

When he reaches for the blindfold he is struck again across the face, a heavy slap that staggers him. His head spins. Hands pull him up straight. The strength of their grip is frightening. It is a man, he thinks, because of the strength of the hands and the fact that its breath comes from slightly above him. But it is a thing even if it is a man, and Nathan is afraid of it, because it is as if it has always been waiting for him, as if it always knew he would come.

The thing pulls Nathan's arms behind him and shoves him forward. It twists Nathan's arms to control him, and they walk. There is no sense of hurry. Nothing is said. Nathan feels as if they have come to a lighter place, as if there is moonlight, but he knows better than to touch the blindfold. His arms hurt, but he tries to make as little sound as possible. They come to stairs and climb. These are different stairs than before, and the feeling of a narrow space. They are climbing for a long time, they change direction twice. Nathan can feel the thing's bare body, its hairy front. Finally they stop climbing, and the thing shoves him, twisting his arms.

One arm lights with pain, and Nathan makes a small sound because of it. He stumbles forward and crashes into something soft, he hits his head on a bar and sinks into softness, the smell of cloth, the rasp of a button on his cheek. The impression of a button is clear. His knee strikes the corner of something hard. Before he can stand on his own, the hands are pulling him, he is jerked by the shoulders, and again the strength of the man-thing surprises him. He is turned around to face it and he is trembling.

"Please don't hit me any more. I won't touch the blindfold. I won't run."

He can hear the moistness of its lips. It is wetting its lips with its tongue. Something about the darkness, the fact that Nathan cannot see, makes the sound seem familiar, and for a moment he is afraid this is Dad, Dad has followed him here.

A hand cups Nathan's jaw, applying no pressure, simply framing the jaw. Nathan holds perfectly still.

The other hand rips the blindfold free.

It has been tied so tight up till now. Everything is a blur. The outline of the man-thing faces him. Shoulders squared, breath heaving. The face still hidden in shadow. They are in the attic, they are under a low-pitched roof. Objects appear in a haze: a heap of white fabric, a chair leg, a broom. Nathan rubs his eyes gently. He is seeing better and better. The man stands behind him. He is wearing jeans. He wears no shirt, and his body is thick and powerful. Moonlight from a dormer window coats his flesh in milk and shadow.

Nathan should recognize the body, the roundness and brownness of nipples nested among dense hair. But Nathan is dazed and the shadow face will not resolve, the body steps forward and pulls a narrow bottle from its back pocket. Eyes that have been struck by lightning, they glitter. "You want some whiskey, Nathan?"

"No."

"You sure? It might calm you down."

"I'm all right."

The voice jangles. Nathan should know it. "We went through that first bottle too fast. I'm keeping this one to myself. You know what I mean?"

He swallows. The long relaxed motion of his throat catches moonlight, shimmers. He keeps his eyes on Nathan as he drinks.

Setting the bottle on the floor nearby, he grabs Nathan by the shirt and wipes his mouth on it. Nathan tries to pull away, and a fist hits him again. The impact of the hand is as sudden as before, and Nathan feels thunder and staggers.

"Don't pull away from me." There is something plaintive in his voice, almost soft. But then there are his eyes, blazing like a predator cat. "Don't."

"Okay. I won't."

Silence again. A glazed look in Burke's eyes. It is Burke, that is the name. But for a moment it is like a shadow taking Burke's shape. Burke has not decided what to do, not entirely. He shrugs his shoulders, and Nathan realizes how much bigger than Roy he actually is. His body has a frightening hardness. He focuses on Nathan again. "Roy left you in the house."

Silence.

"I came back." His fingers dig into Nathan's shoulders. "You don't like me, do you?"

"I like you fine."

"Do you?"

"Yes."

Burke wets his lips. "I saw you."

Nathan's heart picks up its beat. "You did?"

"Oh yeah. You were on the floor. You know when?"

"When?"

"When Roy had your dick in his mouth. When he was on his knees in front of you and he was sucking your dick. Do you suck his dick too?"

Nathan feels a throbbing in his head, and a heaviness in all his limbs. He speaks past the weight on his chest. "It wasn't like that. He wasn't doing that."

"Yes he was."

"Please, Burke, let's go back to camp—"

But this enrages Burke, and he shakes Nathan violently, then shoves him against the low roof. Nathan bangs his head again and collapses. He is a heap on the floor, rising up on his arms, as Burke looms over him. "We ain't going nowhere." He is unbuttoning and unzipping his jeans and stepping out of them furiously. A shadow plays over his bare arms and thighs. Nathan tries to stand and Burke says, "If you move from that spot I'll kill you right now."

He flings down the jeans. He stands there breathing. Nathan, dazed, can hardly keep him in focus. But the mass of him is there, waiting.

"That hurt you? When I pushed you?"

Nathan shakes his head.

"You do like I say, I won't hurt you."

Silence.

"You hear me?"

"Yes."

"You going to do like I say?"

"Yes."

He can focus now. A blur resolves to the motion of arms and legs, Burke standing over him, jerking him up by the shirt collar. Then rough motion ensues, that Nathan hardly follows, and his face is crushed against Burke, against fabric that smells of sweat; then Burke shoves his undershorts down his thighs and pushes his cock against Nathan's lips.

The house has become silent again. Burke looks down at Nathan, at Nathan's mouth, at his own hand around his cock. He runs his free hand roughly through

Nathan's hair, then cups the back of Nathan's head. "You better do it."

Weariness. The hollow place in Nathan is echoing now, the inner wind is ripping him to rags, entering through the place where Dad tore him, the opening that Burke sees now, the wound that does not close. The dark attic fills with the sound that only Nathan can hear, the one note of the one song. He has knelt in this way before, there is nothing to do but let go again, with his head throbbing. It is as if he deserves it, as if both he and Burke understand that he is made for this use. There is a hole in Nathan, and Burke can see it; Dad opened a hole in Nathan, and now anyone can use it. He opens his mouth, he makes a circle. Burke pushes inside.

Burke is rough and clumsy. Worse, an urgency, a need to burn, fills him, and he batters Nathan. Nathan gags and can hardly get air, but Burke's hand at the back of his head forces him to remain. Burke is very excited and breathes like a bellows. His body stiffens and presses spasmodically against Nathan. The skin smells of alcohol and sweat. Nathan focuses, as he learned to do with his father, on the small details, on the curling of a particular hair or the slight ridge of a vein. With Dad he learned not to close his eyes, it made Dad mad. But Dad could make a lot of noise, Burke is silent. He squeezes Nathan's head and there is something fierce in the pressure, added to the sudden thrust of Burke's groin, and the thing in Nathan's mouth swells up. Burke thrashes and gasps, shoving himself against Nathan's face. The hand hurts. Burke pushes him back to the floor and pounds himself against Nathan, banging his head on the floorboards, till Nathan is nearly unconscious.

But then he is thrown again, across something, roughly. He is reminded of Burke's strength, of the feeling of uncontrollable fury in him. When Nathan is still again, he kneels against a wooden beam. Burke comes behind him, jerking Nathan's shirt up his shoulders. Nathan's pants are already around his knees. Burke fumbles with Nathan's undershorts, ripping them before he slides the elastic across Nathan's buttocks. The sense of nakedness is keen. With his hand he is guiding himself into Nathan from behind, spitting into his palm and rubbing the spit on his cock. Nathan recognizes the sound, the motion. He tries to go away. There is no reason to run, it will end, it always does. But Burke is rougher than Dad, and when he enters it is as if he wants to make Nathan hurt, everything is tearing. Nathan whimpers a little and tries to push Burke off; but Burke wraps Nathan with both arms and slams into him. He is making harsh sounds and moving furiously, saying words Nathan can hardly hear. The feeling of violence swells, and Burke shoves his face to the floor, begins to pound it with his fist from behind, slamming hard, over and over again. He releases Nathan as he comes. Nathan lies perfectly still on the floor. His face is bloody, and he cannot open one eye. Burke whimpers as he pulls free of Nathan. He stares down at himself. His body is rigid, every muscle corded. His face is one wash of misery as he stares down, at nothing. He groans. His fist crashes down once, onto Nathan's gut; Nathan doubles over, chokes and gasps. Then something else flashes. Burke lifts the chairleg like a club. He tests the weight in his hand. He swings. He swings again.

It surprises Nathan, that he can hear his own skull crack. The last motion he sees is the chair leg falling into the center of his face. A hole opens up in his head, and the wind touches his brain. He is never sure when Burke leaves, whether he dresses first or carries his clothes. The night lasts a long time. He cannot rest.

Chapter Thirteen

After daylight Roy and Randy find him. Sun enters through the same windows that admitted moonlight the night before, and a bar of sunlight falls straight across Nathan. But he is still cold. He wishes for a blanket. There might be something in the room, he remembers falling into cloth, but he is too sore to move.

Roy's shadow crosses the attic floorboards. He stands there looking at Nathan. There is something ridiculous about him, it is really funny that Roy can look so helpless like this. He simply stands there. Randy comes up behind him and looks down and says, "Jesus." He stares at Nathan too. Somehow this all seems natural, even the fact that Nathan cannot move, cannot find his mouth, cannot acknowledge them. Then Randy heaves and doubles up and turns. Roy kneels. Touching Nathan's arm as he has done many times. Perfectly blank and listless, staring at the air over Nathan's head, he shakes his head once, as if to clear it.

Randy says, "Jesus. He's dead, ain't he? Just like Burke said."

"His arm is cold."

"Look at his face."

Roy swallows. Tears are sliding down his cheeks. "Find something to cover him up. I can't stand to see him lying here like this."

"I swear, I can't look at him."

"Get me that cloth over there. Hand it to me. You don't have to look at him."

He sits there. His eyes are glazed. He takes the cloth from behind. With careful gentleness he spreads the fabric over Nathan, tucking it around his feet, across his shoulders. "I don't want to cover your face."

"What?" Randy asks.

"Nothing." He stands. His voice cascades downward. "You better go ahead with Burke. You better go now and get a head start."

"You think it happened like Burke said?"

"I don't trust nothing Burke said. Go on. Now."

Randy slides away. A long time passes. Roy sits against one of the posts, tucked tight into a ball. After a while this is almost comfortable, and even this seems natural to Nathan, who is still cold, who still cannot move.

Chapter Fourteen

He has the sense of lines dividing once more, of himself as if he is sleeping, peaceful as if he is lying on a shore listening to the waves of a sea.

He has gotten confused. There are people in the house, more than he can count, passing beneath in the corridors and outside along the porches. Voices of people everywhere, on every side, black voices and white voices, echoing.

He cannot tell whether time is passing or whether he is lying in it perfectly still.

Roy is hovering above him. Nathan knows it is a memory and he should not open himself to that. But he lets himself see Roy, the clean sad face hanging like a cloud.

Then his father replaces Roy, who has disappeared. Dad jerks the cloth off Nathan. It is a cold day, Nathan is very cold now, he is not sure what day it is, and Dad is taking off the cloth that keeps him warm. Flashlights are trained on Nathan to augment afternoon light. Dad is not alone, there are other voices, other men, and the crackling of a radio. Dad is looking down at him. This is not a memory but something else. Can Dad see the hole? Surely he can.

For a moment fear returns, as vivid as in the house in Rose Hill. It is as if this is the father of that night, a long time ago, with that father's younger bones and smoother skin. He with his flat belly and strong hands leans over Nathan, and there is something tender and sorrowful in his expression. Nathan wonders how Dad got here. Nathan wonders what Dad will want to do this time. Will it make any difference that Nathan has a hole in his skull?

But instead, Dad places the cloth over him tenderly. It is like a vision from some time in the future, or like something out of a dream. Dad covers Nathan's face with the gauzy cloth and Nathan is grateful for the thought of the quiet whiteness that waits beneath it. Except, just at the moment the cloth settles over him forever, he sees Roy waiting behind Dad, his face emerging out of the shadow, drawn and gaunt. The sight fills Nathan with a longing he can hardly contain.

He will shake his head to free himself. He has practiced the gesture for most of his life, he will find it easy. When he does, he will be in the present again, and he will be awake, and Dad will be nowhere near. He will shake his head, and sit up in the attic, and find Roy.

Chapter Fifteen

His mouth is dry and his lips are caked with blood.

The soft glow of early morning fills the attic. Light outlines the angled roof, ceiling beams, old boxes, an open steamer trunk littered with ratshit.

He stands carefully. His joints are stiff and sore but the pain is not so much.

Kneeling slowly, he peers out a window that offers a view of the side yard facing the barn, the path leading to the slave houses.

His head aches. When he touches it the flesh is very sore and tender. Blood is caked in clumps in his hair.

The bottle of liquor stands on the floor, in the same place where Burke left it. There is still liquor in the bottle.

Where he was lying, by the support beam, more blood has dried, in the vague outline of himself.

Is he trapped here? At first he is afraid he will not be able to leave the attic. But he finds the exit easily. The doorknob, solid to his touch, turns, he opens the door and descends.

Chapter Sixteen

The attic stair leads him down to the second story. The adjacent service stair has been boarded shut, and he can descend no further in that direction. So he picks a path down the upstairs corridors. He finds rooms from the night before. He finds the doll's foot, clean and shining. He finds the chair facing the fireplace, the room flooded with light, the stain on the fabric clearly outlined. Nathan descends in perfect silence along the grand staircase into the vaulted foyer with the water pooled at the bottom, the fallen floor sagging toward earth. The room seems very beautiful and sweetly perfumed. Nathan wanders along the walls, careful of where he steps. He slips through the parlor, the library, into the back of the house, the ball-room with its sealed windows, the adjacent service rooms. Daylight trickles through the shutters. Ivy crawls the inner walls.

He finds the place they must have hidden, he and Roy. The room is plain and ordinary, a bedroom or even a storeroom. Smaller than it seemed in the dark. Something about the place draws him to stay. He stands where he stood when Roy knelt in front of him.

He explores further, rooms they missed when they were wandering in the dark. The house is larger than it seems. He has the feeling he could wander here, for a long time, so he is very careful to keep his bearings. The empty house welcomes him, yields itself to him. He visits the service rooms in the rear, the wrecked dining room, rooms that seem to have no purpose at all. But the end of his wanderings find him where he meant to be, in the room on the second floor where the tree has fallen against the house.

He stands near the open window, taking deep breaths of fresh air. His head is clearing. There is only one way to find out if he can leave the house, he sticks his head through the window, pushes with his arms, crawls over the sill. Aside from the fact that his limbs are stiff and sore, he exits without hindrance. He stands on the porch breathing the brisk morning air, autumn in the woods.

Chapter Seventeen

He walks through the garden at the side of the house. Many more of the flowers are blooming in the yard than he remembers from the day before, the garden a mix of well-tended and wild. There are evening primrose, senna, asters, verbena, elecampane, gay feather, spiderflower, goldenrod, cone flowers, bottle gentian, ironweed, queen-of-the-meadow, boneset, yarrow, cornflowers, false foxglove, turtleheads, and sunflowers. Names learned from his mother, remembered vividly. For a time he wonders if he will find her wandering here, reciting these names to herself. This would be her place. But the garden is deserted. He meanders among the wild flowerbeds, searching for the gate.

Morning sun floods the front yard. Out there is the creek and the place where they camped.

He walks to the campsite. His progress is slow at first, his limbs resist every motion, as if cracking, breaking, with each step. But the sunlight helps, and so does the cool creek water, bathing his cracked lips. He soaks his hair but can only begin to get rid of the blood. The ache of cold water on the bone is unendurable. The campsite is deserted. It might have been used a hundred years ago. Yet the ashes in the circle are still warm.

Chapter Eighteen

He leaves the vicinity of the house. It is as if he has been walking for a century at least. Down the remnants of Poke's Road he passes the uprooted tree. Soon he leaves sight of the lane of sentinel oaks, retracing the path of the morning walk that seems so long ago.

He rests in the clearing where Burke took off his shirt and drank liquor. He walks near the creek there, haunting the place. He soaks more of the dried blood from his hair. Feeling almost presentable again.

This is the place where he will meet Burke. Never in the attic, only here. Confused, pacing up and down the bank of the dark creek, Burke will be watching the road. It will be his image, it will always linger. It will wait for Nathan, it will wish for Roy. It will take off its shirt, it will be a man.

Chapter Nineteen

At the place where the boys camped for the night during the storm, Nathan sits under the tree at the edge of the clearing where they cooked and told stories. The rock circle at the center of the clearing holds the ghost of the fire. The blue of the sky has begun to deepen with clouds, as if a storm is coming. In the tremulous wind he kneels at the creek to bathe again. With careful motion he cleans his swollen lips, his bruised face. His hair feels soft and supple in his fingertips.

He rests again on the Indian mound later in the afternoon, sitting at the top where the grassy summit sails above the treetops. He can see all the way to the western horizon, the royal purple of the clouded sky, a sliver of sun behind the clouds that bursts into a piercing ray.

The mound is a haven, and there Nathan feels less alone. The calm green of the grass restores itself as the storm clouds thin and the sun swells again. It is easy to be here. The mound as a place of memory offers safety; he can remember the first time Roy brought him here. He can linger there, in that space of day as he remembers it. He can safely remember many things about Roy, he can even remember Roy turning his back and walking away. It was only once, only one time.

But the thought of Roy makes him restless. Finding Roy. Though Nathan is very tired now, he stands again, ignoring the fierce pain in his legs.

Chapter Twenty

In the late afternoon he comes to the clearing that leads to the pond. He walks through the cemetery, past the cherub and his stubby wings, along the pond's edge. He keeps to the forest, walking the long way round the far end of the pond. He stops close to the houses. The yards are empty, eerie quiet emanating from beyond. The schoolbus sits under the trees. Dad's car is out of sight.

A woman stands on each of the porches. Each is looking into the woods, as if she has lost something there. Nathan recognizes his own mother, and Roy's. Roy's mother wears the faded blue apron Nathan has seen before. She crosses the yard to dump a pan of scraps into the compost heap near one corner of the barn. Her large body moves with rolling steps, in waves of fat. She returns to stand at the door again, her expression again obscured by the screen.

Nathan's own mother keeps her vigil further back, leaning on the doorjamb with the kitchen visible behind her. She hovers in shadow, and Nathan sees little more than her silhouette and stance. But he recognizes her by the crooked way she crosses her arms, one hand dangling loose. She carries the familiar aura of weariness, of having a veil over her vision. But he can feel her searching. She has not forgotten.

Nathan remains hidden in the shadow at the edge of the trees. Wondering why Roy's mother is searching. Wondering whether Roy ever came home.

Chapter Twenty-One

He has no clear image of where he is headed as a final destination until he hears the music through the trees. It is late. The storm has cleared but the sun is low. A thin thread of piano and organ, "Blessed Redeemer, Jesus Is Mine" drifts from beyond.

Ahead, where the forest abruptly stops, the slanted sunlight falls very clear and bright. A green lawn slopes downward to where another creek flows, nestled among shaggy cedars. In the lap of that lawn a white church blazes, its sharp steeple rising above a broad oak.

Nathan waits at the top of the slope, hidden among the trees. Down the hill a lot of cars are parked in the grass, and people dressed like Sunday evening stand in the yard. The service has ended, and people are coming out of the sanctuary. The music continues, "Just As I Am, without One Plea." No one is singing, only the piano and organ play.

Then out of the church comes Roy.

Chapter Twenty-Two

He has been crying. A girl in a white dress walks with him. They move slowly, as if they are underwater, and for a moment Nathan is mesmerized by the sight. A preacher talks in Roy's ear, offering comfort. The girl in the white dress strokes Roy's hair. The fact of the church service has lent her radiance; the white dress makes Nathan think this is their wedding, but no, there are no other signs, no car decorated with streamers, no showers of dry rice. It is only a white dress. Here is Evelyn with Roy.

Roy lifts his head.

Now a lot of people crowd the churchyard. The sky over the steeple is flushing pink. When Nathan steps out of the woods, they all see him.

Nobody knows him but Roy. For a moment he can only stand there.

Roy releases Evelyn's arm, gently insistent. He walks toward Nathan with only a little hesitation. She follows him for a few steps. It may be that she calls his name, but there is a lot of noise in the churchyard, as the piano strikes up "Standing on the Promises."

Roy calmly walks toward Nathan. When he is close enough to be sure of what he sees, he runs.

Chapter Twenty-Three

He stops a few feet away. His heart is visibly pounding, fear and confusion surround him. He finds his voice with some effort. His eyes are glittering. "How did you get here?"

"I walked."

Someone else must have recognized Nathan, other people are starting to approach them now. Nathan reaches for Roy's hand but at the last moment is afraid to touch it. He backs away.

The motion makes Roy desperate. "Stop. Where are you going?"

"I don't think I can stay here."

"Stop. Please." His eyes are bright and glittering. He looks behind, at the shining church, at the scattering of people approaching across the lawn. Nathan retreats another few steps and Roy stumbles toward him. He reaches, arms out. "I didn't mean to leave you. I went back to that room but you were gone. Please don't go away again."

They are close. At first Nathan can hardly feel anything, can hardly feel Roy's hands. But then he can feel the warmth, and he can smell Roy's breath. And suddenly Nathan is certain he still has a body: because he can feel Roy near him, can smell the sweetness of his clean hair, his fresh-shaven mustache. Suddenly they are embracing each other, disregarding everything that has happened, disregarding even the crowd of other people as they approach.

They face each other. The moment lengthens—the green of evening, the clear piano, the freshness of the white dress. The sweetness of living. Nathan waits and watches.

Finally he asks the question that has made him afraid all this time. "How long have I been gone?"

"Today." Roy can hardly form the words. "We left you today. The sheriff just went back with your dad. To get you." He breaks off, watching Nathan.

He is understanding, now. He is choosing. He looks deep into the trees.

Nathan turns and breaks into a gait between a limp and a trot. After a moment, silent, Roy follows, and takes his hand.

It is a relief that they can feel each other, that their hands are warm. It is a relief that they are in the same world. They disappear into the woods.

Chapter Twenty-Four

They stop to rest a little way inside the forest, under a gingko tree, its golden leaves showering around them as they get their breath. They have arrived on the evening when all of the gingko leaves will fall, leaving the tree naked as a skeleton. The tree stands in a open glade, catching the last shreds of light. Nathan says he needs to sit for a minute, and Roy says fine, and they sit, with the gingko leaves piling slowly around them, a snowdrift of saffron and amber.

They keep very quiet, listening for sounds of pursuit. Roy slides an arm around Nathan's shoulders. Nathan feels all the reticence with which the gesture is performed, then sighs and leans against Roy. "You were dead," Roy says, but his tone is more of confiding than disapproving. "I saw you."

"I know."

They are aware, especially, of their own warmth in the pile of leaves.

"What do we do now?"

"Run away."

The notion of leaving hovers, they breathe it in. Roy examines the wound in Nathan's skull, a distracted quality to his scrutiny, as if he is seeing another picture. The image of fresher blood.

"Anyhow. Our preacher preached this evening about how the dead will rise." Roy drops his Bible into the grass. "I guess we could go up north somewhere."

The words drift skyward. They sit till they are half-buried in gold leaves. Roy's white shirt gleams. He pulls Nathan against him and for a while they become one flesh. Roy is rapt, as if he is singing inside. Or maybe it is more as if he is blossoming, a flower opening at this very moment. Nathan remembers, oddly, Preacher John Roberts leaning over the pulpit toward the congregation in puzzlement, in confusion at the notion of the Disciple John resting his head on Jesus's chest. Nathan rests his head there on Roy and understands. In the distance they hear the voices of people searching for them in the woods. They stand and go. They never look back.